Algebra and Demons

By Vik Azeem

1987

"Are you ready to dance?"

Sandra looked at David in his shining suit and then peered at her own high heels glittering in the strobe lights.

"I think so", she answered uneasily.

The annual Dale Bridge High homecoming dance had begun an hour prior. The auditorium was draped in autumn decorations set up by the Homecoming club. Immaculate card board trees with paper leaves hanging off the side sat next to a wooden stage where the DJ turned discs at the request of the students.

David and Sandra stepped out onto the dance floor to both smiling approval and transparent jealousy from the other students. The opinions of them were polarizing, as was the case with all the popular kids in school. There was no doubt that they ranked highest in the hierarchy of couples at Dale Bridge High.

The turnout is pretty much as I expected, Sandra thought to herself. The big question on her mind was whether or not she was going to be elected homecoming queen. The competition was rough, with two other senior cheerleaders running and also a prominent member of the school's volleyball team.

Still, her friends had insisted all week that she was the favorite. It was likely her relationship with David that had put her at the front of the pack.

"You look handsome tonight", she said to David as they danced.

"I know."

Sandra laughed at his response. But inside she was already experiencing the same thought that had clouded her mind for days.

Did David and she have any real future together?

They had met a year ago at a local social gathering. She wasn't much of a party person but she had realized quickly that it came with the territory of being head cheerleader. On that particular night, David had won her over by doing a karaoke version of the Michael Jackson song 'Ben.'

They had been inseparable ever since. But recently she couldn't help but feel that she had lost some of her own identity during the course of the relationship.

Who am I?

She had contemplated that question at the start of the year and struggled for an answer.

She was head cheerleader, yes, but she had long suspected that there had to be more to life than social status. She had picked up art as a hobby during the summer, and taken a huge interest in the great artists of the past. Her personal favorite was Vincent Van Gough. But David didn't seem to share any enthusiasm for her new interest.

After a slow song had run its course, the DJ grabbed the microphone.

"Alright party people, I have a special treat for you. One of the year's biggest hits! Jefferson Starship, 'Nothings Gonna Stop Us Now.'

"What a groovy song!" David said as he grabbed Sandra and started dancing a little bit quicker than her heels liked.

Sandra wanted to enjoy the moment, but she couldn't stop herself from continuing to worry about what lied ahead. Any time she tried to talk to David about the future he changed the subject. Somehow they usually ended up gossiping about other popular kids in school.

They had radically different plans for the future. David wanted to go to a party school, while she wanted to go to a private college that was more academic oriented.

She listened to the lyrics of the song as they boomed in her ear.

"Looking in your eyes, I see a paradise. This world that I've found, it's too good to be true."

Maybe he'll mature in time, Sandra thought hopefully. *How many guys in high school are serious about the future? He'll grow out of it.*

"Let the world around us, just fall apart. Baby we can make it if we're heart to heart!"

Her feet began to hurt at that very moment. She cursed herself for not wearing dance shoes.

She leaned into David's ear. "I need to stop. My feet are ready to fall off."

David nodded and then led her off the dance floor to the wall on the side of the auditorium.

"I'm sorry I didn't dress for the part."

"Forget about it." David responded. "Did you see everybody looking at us? The throne is ours."

"But why would you want it?" Sandra heard a voice say suddenly.

She turned and saw a familiar face leaning against the wall next to them.

"What did you say Dick?" David asked.

"It's Don."

"Whatever."

Sandra noticed right away that Don was dressed in his usual white t-shirt and jeans. Sandra could see others on the dance floor whispering and laughing about him. But Don didn't seem to care.

"Why would anybody not want to be homecoming king and queen?" Sandra asked.

Don laughed again.

"Dearest Sandra, you must realize that life is so much bigger than this."

David nodded. ""Sure it is Don. Now why don't you go solve world hunger and leave us alone?"

Don didn't move.

"You guys want a better reason? I have one. You know the whole worrying about popularity thing? It is not a big fan of that."

Sandra raised an eye curiously.

"It?"

Don leaned in close to Sandra.

"I'm not talking about some crazy clown from a Stephen King novel either."

"So what are you talking about?"

"You want to know?"

"Yes."

"Magra", he said with a whisper.

David sighed.

"I am really not in the mood to hear this Twilight Zone nonsense."

Don turned his attention to David.

"Hey brother, Judd Nelson from the Breakfast Club called. He wants his personality back."

David put his hands together and cracked his knuckles.

"Why don't you just beat your feet?"

"Because I don't know what that means?"

"Go kick rocks loser."

"Loser? Gee, that's a big word for you David. You are moving up in the vocabulary world."

"What is Magra?" Sandra asked.

"That would be the name of our local demon."

"Demon?"

"I'm sure you know the story."

"I don't."

"Demons are supernatural beings that have the power to possess the world of the living. And we have one right here in Dale Bridge."

"That is nothing but a fairy tale", David said.

Don stared at the ground.

"My father never told me any fairy tales. He did however teach me how to hunt."

"There are no such things as demons", Sandra said.

David gave Don a slight nudge in the chest.

"This deadbeat here gets off on trying to scare people."

Don took a step forward, than thought better of it and took a step back

"Believe what you wish brother. But don't say I didn't warn you."

"I should warn you that I'm probably going to hit you in the face if you don't leave."

Don smiled suddenly and began to walk away.

"Have a great time tonight quarterback."

"What was all that demon stuff he was talking about?"

"Who knows", David answered quickly. "Hey listen, how about instead of dinner tonight at the Apple Pit we just hang out in my basement? My parents will be asleep so we'll have privacy."

"And what do we need that for?"

"To play Battleship of course. What do you think?"

"David, we talked about sexual intercourse."

"Sandra, it's the eighties. Nobody calls it sexual intercourse anymore."

"I'm just not ready yet."

"What makes you think my plan was to seduce you?"

"David, you've never once invited me to your basement before."

"Well I only now just cleaned it. Ok, the truth is it's still not clean. But, I thought maybe you could help me clean it."

"I don't understand."

"Look, I don't want you to think I'm trying to seduce you."

"That's usually what happens in movies."

"Yeah but what does that John Hughes fellow know anyways?"

"So you're not still hung up on the sex thing?"

"Well I don't see why it's such a big a deal. Everybody else is comfortable with it."

"You shouldn't always go with the crowd."

"So you would really rather eat apple pie tonight?"

"Why didn't you bring this up earlier instead of proposing it at the last minute?"

David stood against the wall and fidgeted nervously as he put his hand through his hair.

"I didn't think about it like that."

"We're graduating high school, David. You have to start making decisions like an adult. And I'm not talking about Subway or Taco Bell."

He backed away from the wall suddenly.

"Could you stop using my name so much? My mom does that, it's really annoying."

"I'm sorry. I just want you to think about the future."

David punched the wall suddenly.

"Screw the future. I'm going to go get some punch."

She watched him walk over to the opposite side of the auditorium where the punch was. He poured himself a cup and didn't waste any time taking a big sip.

I really hope the punch bowl isn't spiked, Sandra thought. The last thing she needed was for David to be angry and drunk.

She turned her attention from David to a boy walking towards her.

Reece Hicks.

She had been making frequent small talk with him in English during the last few weeks. He approached with a smile and took a place next to her against the wall. Sandra noticed his broad shoulders just as she had the first time she met him in class. She figured he probably could have been on one of the sports teams if he had tried out.

"I have a question for you", he said.

"What is it?"

"Have you noticed how many inconsistencies there are in the English language?"

"I guess I never took the time to think about it."

"Let me give you an example. Look at the word incredible. Shouldn't it be the opposite of the word credible? Shouldn't it mean to lack in credibility?"

"That's a good point. Maybe you should write a letter to somebody?"

"I plan too."

They both stood back and listened to the Michael Jackson song 'The Way You Make Me Feel'.

"Are you having fun?" He asked.

"I was, how about you?"

"I'm waiting for the DJ to play the song 'Africa' by Toto. He's played everything except that."

"It is a great song."

"Yeah, so it's none of my business, but I saw you and David arguing."

She looked at David working on his second cup of punch.

"Sometimes I can't conversate with him at all."

"You mean converse."

"Oh, right. You read a lot don't you?"

"I'm really into Stephen King."

"I heard his books are long."

"You can't rush quality."

"Maybe I'll try reading one. I used to go out with David all the time, but lately I've been staying inside and reading more."

"If you don't mind me saying, I don't think you two are similar at all."

"What do you mean?"

Reece looked over at David.

"Well, I've been in classes with both of you. David, he's a doodler. Now, there is nothing wrong with doodling, it's fun, it's easy, and it kills time."

He paused for a moment and then looked at her again.

"You, on the other hand, are somebody who participates in class. You drive discussions, organize projects, and lead groups. You're the kind of person that goes above and beyond what's required."

Sandra couldn't help but smile. It was rare that any guy complimented her on anything academic related.

"The girl I see in my English class, that girl has nothing in common with that guy over there drinking punch. They live in two different stratospheres."

"But they say opposites attract."

"I think that phrase was meant to pertain to food, not relationships. You know, like Peanut Butter and Jelly."

""What are you doing when school ends Reece?"

"Military."

"I thought you would be going to college?"

"I will eventually. It's just that my parents don't have any money. The military will give me a full ride through school."

"Wow, you really plan for the future."

"My dad always says the future is what you make it. Listen, I better go. There is a guy over there who wants to discuss whether or not Catcher in the Rye is as good as all our teachers say."

"Do you think it is?"

"Why don't you come over and join us?"

Sandra didn't immediately respond. She hadn't expected the conversation with Reece to interest her so much, but now she was questioning herself.

What do I do? If she walked around with Reece, David would go crazy.

She finally shook her head.

"I can't. But will you be around later after the king and queen ceremony?"

She wasn't ignoring her feelings so much as pushing them to the side.

"I was thinking about going home and watching Plains, Trains, and Automobiles. But I'll probably be around."

He turned to leave but she called out to him.

"The book was revolutionary for its time."

"Sorry?"

She smiled. "I wanted to give you my thoughts on the Catcher and the Rye."

"Oh. We are in agreement about that. Hey, can you do me a favor?"

"Yes?"

"Save me a dance."

"Count on it."

She watched him walk away.

What do I have to do to get a girl like that? It was a thought that ran through Reece's mind as he stood by the punch bowl. *She's smart, kind hearted, and has a clear picture of what she wants in the future. There aren't too many girls like that around here.*

It wasn't long before Reece was blaming himself.

I waited too long to talk to her.

He had seen her in the hallways and the library throughout the four years of high school. But he had only had the courage to talk to her when she happened to be sitting in front of him in English that year.

At least I may get to dance with her tonight.

"You want to dance with her, don't you"?

Somebody had read his mind. Reece turned to see Don Cramers standing with a curious smile.

"How did you know that?"

"I saw you talking with her earlier."

"She has a boyfriend."

"Many lovers have overcome far greater obstacles. Besides, he is a stupid idiot. The likes of which would never stand a chance against true love."

"True Love? I barely even know her."

"That's a minor and quite frankly insignificant detail."

"Don, who are you?"

"Just someone who sees things for what they are."

Reece looked out on the floor and noticed that a lot of the kids were stumbling as they danced.

"Whoever spiked the punch bowl is probably laughing it up right about now."

Don looked around.

"Whoever did it is a genius. This whole dance is just a bunch of zombies walking around aimlessly."

"That's harsh. What do you have against everybody?"

Don looked around and shook his head.

"This town, it wasn't meant for the happy."

"What is wrong with Dale Bridge?"

"There are things that I can't elaborate on."

"That really clears it up for me, thanks."

"Trust me on this brother. The best thing you can do for your future is to make Dale Bridge your past."

Reece nodded slowly and looked up at the clock. It was close to the time when the King and Queen would be announced.

"Don, I…" Reece stopped talking when he saw that Don was gone.

He looked around the room but couldn't place him anywhere.

He is a strange one.

The school principal Mr. Shavers held the microphone and had everyone's attention an hour later. Reece stood against the wall in the back watching as the rest of the students waited in anticipation for the announcement of homecoming king and queen.

Reece spotted David and Sandra in the front. David looked stoked, but Reece could have sworn that Sandra looked upset about something.

"Hello students", Mr. Shavers began. "I want to thank you all for attending tonight's dance. Now it is the moment you have been waiting for. Can I have a drumroll please?"

The DJ on cue played a drumroll.

"This year's homecoming king and queen are…"

A hush silence fell across the crowd.

"David Voorhees and Sandra Myers!"

There was a huge round of applause as Reece saw Sandra and David walk up onto the stage towards the podium.

"Congrats", Mr. Shavers said as he handed them each a crown.

David excitedly put the crown on but Sandra just stood there with the crown in her hand. She looked out into the crowd and for a brief moment made eye contact with Reece.

She doesn't look happy, Reece thought to himself.

David and Sandra stepped to the side of the stage and began posing for pictures.

Reece began to make his way towards the stage, figuring he would talk to Sandra.

She still owes me a dance.

He was about half way to the front when he heard a piercing scream to the right of him.

What the hell?

He turned and saw Mandy Patkins fall to the ground.

There was blood leaking from her dress onto the dance floor.

Reece looked up and saw her boyfriend Kip holding a pocket sized knife in his hand.

"Kip! Put the knife down" Reece heard someone scream.

Kip responded by turning to his left and immediately stabbing Jenny Jenkins in the back.

Jenny screamed in pain and fell lifeless to the ground.

Reece saw a very crazy look in Kip's eyes as all the students in the gym began scattering towards the exit. At that moment Kip began stabbing any student that ran by him.

"Why is the door locked??" Reece heard someone else scream.

We're all locked in. Reece thought to himself. *This is going to be bad.*

Reece thought about it only a second longer before deciding to attack Kip.

He wisely approached from an unseen angle and caught Kip off guard.

Kip yelled out in surprise and they both fell to the floor. Reece saw the knife fly out of Kip's hand and slide across the floor.

"Will someone open this damn door?" The principal yelled out.

Reece than grabbed Kip by the collar and yelled at him.

"What the hell is wrong with you?"

Reece was shocked to see fear and confusion in Kip's eyes.

"What are you talking about man?" Kip answered.

"You just started stabbing people!"

It seemed like a revelation to Kip who shook his head in amazement.

"No! I couldn't have! I was just over there drinking punch!"

Reece let go of his collar and looked to where the knife had slid.

He started to go after it, but he saw David pick it up.

Reece stood and called to him.

"David, what are you doing with the knife?"

David had an odd look in his eye as he shrugged.

He then turned around and stabbed the DJ in his throat.

"What the hell!" Reece screamed.

The DJ fell to the ground, dead. David laughed.

"Now where is my sweet Sandra?" He said.

Reece quickly surveyed the room and spotted Sandra making her way towards the exit along with one of her friends. Reece quickly surmised that she was putting herself in a dead end. He looked at David who had noticed Sandra at the exact same time.

Reece started running towards the exit.

He reached Sandra a moment later and grabbed her by the hand.

"Reece! What is going on?"

"I don't know, but I think David is trying to kill you!"

"What?!"

"C'mon! Let's try the back exit, this one is locked."

They made their way through the crowd and started moving towards the back of the auditorium.

Reece couldn't see where David had gone. But he almost gagged at the sight of five fellow students on the ground barely clinging to life.

"Reece, my shoes, I have to take them off!"

"We can't stop! David is here somewhere. We're almost there."

"I don't understand why he is doing this?"

"I don't know, it was Kip at first, but then David picked up the knife."

Reece could see the exit. He figured they would go straight to the police station.

"Reece, I'm sorry I"

She stopped mid-sentence and Reece felt the weight of her hand become heavy as she fell to the ground.

He turned and saw a knife sticking out of her back.

He looked up and saw David standing about fourteen feet away.

The police broke in through the exit door and immediately tackled David to the ground and put cuffs on him.

Reece knelt to the ground and looked at Sandra.

"Sandra, please just hang on. I'll get you to a hospital."

His plea was to no avail. Her eyes were starting to glaze over as she looked back at him. She struggled for a deep breath for a few seconds and then stopped breathing altogether.

"No!" Reece yelled.

The police surrounded him suddenly and an officer spoke into his radio.

"We need an ambulance immediately."

The officer helped Reece up and pushed him away from Sandra's body.

As Reece exited the auditorium he saw both Kip and David being put into the back of a police car. They both shared the same look of confusion. They would both share the claim that something had forced them to kill.

Kip was eventually convicted of murder and sent to prison. David meanwhile committed suicide a few days after the dance. For a while, the school mourned the deaths and wondered what had caused such a horrible event to happen.

But by graduation it was nothing more than a fleeting memory.

Reece couldn't move on so easily. He felt a tremendous sense of guilt for leading Sandra into an open space where David could throw a knife at her. What haunted him was that like the police, he couldn't think of any logical explanation for any of it.

That summer, Reece canceled his plans to join the military and decided to go to a local community college. He found that in his free time he was making frequent trips back to the auditorium, looking for any clues that the police may have missed.

I have to know what really happened.

2

2012

"Which colleges have you applied too?"

I look up from my food and see both my mom and dad staring at me with inquiring minds. The waitress just brought my plate featuring a sizzling sirloin and buttered mashed potatoes. It's a meal that is a perfect combination of taste and aesthetics. But suddenly my appetite has been put on ice.

The unavoidable subject of college always makes me uneasy. My usual response involves me faking enthusiasm about my future prospects. I'm almost good enough to convince myself. As a high school senior, college is the only thing I'm asked about. Nobody seems to care about my opinion on politics. Now I don't actually have an opinion on politics, but it would still be nice to be asked every once in a while.

"Mainly places in state."

"Great", my mom says. "If you get in somewhere close you can stay at home!"

My mom wants me to live at home forever. I suppose there are many moms that feel that way about their only child. My dad interrupts her immediately.

"Honey, we talked about this. He needs to go away for college. It's the only way he's going to become a man."

My dad always likes to talk about me becoming a man. He's one of those fathers that often laments on how he used to walk to school in twelve feet of snow. He also worked two jobs in order to put himself through college while somehow doing an unpaid internship on the side. It's hard not to feel lazy in comparison.

"I just think we could all save money if he stays at home." My mom counters.

I stuff my face with a spoonful of mashed potatoes.

"College isn't about money, it's about the experience", my dad says.

"Well, that explains all of the student loan debt in America."

"Eric, what do you want to do?" My dad turns it back to me.

I cough and swallow the remainder of the potatoes. They usually don't ask me directly.

"I'm not sure", I answer simply.

"But you have to have some opinion on this. Do you want to live in a dorm or stay at home?"

I cough again. I may regret what I'm about to say.

"Are there any other options outside of college?"

There is a brief silence.

"No", they both suddenly answer in perfect unison.

A brave voice deep inside of me makes its way up my spine and through my neck. It articulates itself a second later.

"If everybody went to college, there would be no entertainers or anybody to start a business."

Yes! I don't smile outwardly, but on the inside I am patting myself on the back. I just presented a perfectly logical argument as to why college may not be the definitive choice for me.

"What are you trying to say?" My dad asks.

I have to stay strong and sound confident.

"Well um, you see, the thing is, what I'm trying to say is."

"What is it Eric?"

"Well there are plenty of successful people who don't have degrees. Bill Gates, Steve Jobs, Hulk Hogan, um, William Wallace."

"Who?" My mom asks.

"The guy from Braveheart."

"Eric", my dad says, "do you plan on starting a business?"

"Well, no."

My mom chimes in. "Are you going to be an entertainer?"

"I don't think so."

"So then you're going to college."

Perfectly in-sync. How do they do that?

My parents are obviously set in their ways.

"Eric", my dad says. "You won't really know the importance of college until later on in life."

He's right of course. Maybe my generation does live with an instant gratification mindset. College will probably be very beneficial in the long run. Unfortunately, that type of forethought still doesn't make me want to go.

"Yeah, that's what my guidance counselor says."

"Smart man", my dad says.

They begin talking about politics and I breathe a sigh of relief as I look at the dessert menu.

My parents are right to be excited about me going to college.

The problem is that I don't have the grades for it.

I excuse myself from the table and walk towards the bathroom. I stop upon seeing Samantha, a girl from my school, standing by the counter. She looks a bit worried.

"Hey Samantha, how are you?"

"James, right?"

"Close, it's Eric. I mean I can sort of see how you would mix the two. Are you waiting for an order?"

"No. I'm looking for a ride home."

"Oh."

"My cell phone is dead."

"Will the cashier let you use their phone?"

"He said it's only for paying customers."

"Well I'd let you use mine but the battery is dead."

Actually, I use a pre-paid phone and I'm all out of minutes. She doesn't need to know that.

I look back at the table and see my mom and dad staring at me.

"Hey, I can give you a ride home if you want."

"You have a car?"

"Well I'm here with my mom and dad, but I don't think they would mind."

She looks over at my mom and dad and considers my offer.

"You know, I think I'll be alright. My house is only a few blocks away."

"Are you sure? It's really not a problem."

"Yeah, it's fine."

"Oh, well, alright.

I watch her begin to walk out of the side door.

I call out to her.

"Hey, watch out for Magra." I say jokingly.

"I don't believe in that stuff."

"Neither do I", I say but she's already turned and made her exit.

I return to the table. My mom looks curious.

"Is that your secret girlfriend Eric?"

"Mom, if it was, would I really just talk to her out in the open in front of everyone?"

"So you don't have a girlfriend?"

"No."

"Well why not?"

"I don't know. I just haven't found the right girl."

"Oh. So you are not going to the homecoming dance?"

"How do you know about that?"

"Eric, I wasn't born in the 1700's. Every school has a homecoming dance around this time of the year."

Boy, do I suddenly feel like a loser. There is no worse feeling than when your mom questions why you don't have a girlfriend and why you're not going to the school dance.

"Oh, well I hadn't planned on it."

"Dances are fun honey."

"Yeah, maybe they were in the 80s."

On my way out I notice Dan Fundell and Kenny Winters sitting at a table with a girl I don't know. Dan is somebody I used to play basketball with back in middle school and Kenny has been my friend since we met in drama during my junior year.

I tell my parents I'll be at the car in a few moments.

"Hey, how are you guys?"

"What's the goods bro-ham?" Dan says.

"The goods? Um, well, they are good I guess."

Kenny looks up from his I-Pad. "I haven't seen you at school in a while. Still been skipping?"

"I've had this reoccurring sickness. Listen, are you guys still doing that whole math club thing?"

Dan nods.

"Moshizzle we are."

"Moshizzle?"

"Foshizzle."

"I'm sorry?"

"You have got to get your weight up on the language man."

"Hey Eric, can I borrow the new Madden from you?" Kenny asks.

"Yeah, just stop by my house some time and pick it up. So you guys are really in the math club?"

"This is actually a meeting we're having", Kenny answers.

The girl at the end of the table is looking in the opposite direction through the window so I can't get a clear look of her face. Three people in the math club sounds about right.

"What do you guys do at these meetings?"

"Discuss math related things", Kenny answers quickly.

"Oh, right."

I see a big map laid out on the table.

"Are you sure this is not the Geography club?"

I look closely at the map and see a heading at the top that seems odd.

"Is that a map of the Dale Bridge Cemetery?"

Dan looks at the map than back to me.

"It's just an extra-curricular project that we're working on."

"Well listen, there is a strong possibility that I may need help with Algebra."

Kenny gives a slight chuckle. "You're taking Algebra as a senior?"

"Yeah, what are you taking?"

"Trigonometry."

"Oh. Well I'm sad to say I may actually be failing Algebra, which I can't graduate without."

Dan takes a big sip of his milkshake and then responds. "Word? Yo we may have another meeting in two days if you want to join us."

"Yeah, well, this is all hinges on me getting over my sickness. But I'll keep you updated."

"Get some Nyquil son!"

"Right, I'll look into that, thanks."

3

My alarm clock strikes at seven in the morning. The song, 'Mad World' by Gary Jules plays just loud enough to wake me from a restless slumber. The song is by choice, but the waking up in the morning, that is by force.

Teenagers all across the country are dragging themselves out of bed at this exact moment. Head in the clouds, mind in the gutter, feet touching the floor. It's hard to understand why high school starts so early in the morning.

I roll out of bed and see the DVD cover for 'Pocahontas' lying on the ground next to an unwisely chosen green t-shirt that I haven't worn in four weeks. I had a Disney movie marathon last night, and fell asleep halfway through Pocahontas. I'm pretty curious about what happens at the end.

I guess my life isn't so different from the average high school senior. There are of course the typical teen-angst driven issues that surface in every teen based movie, television show, and novel. I'm not popular, girls don't like me, and I have unexplainable acme. Yes, these are all true. But, those things are too common and trivial for me to actually complain about.

My only real complaint is Algebra.

Man, do I hate Algebra.

I hate it so much that I recently put an ad up on Craigs List for someone to complete my Algebra homework for me. I offered quite a chunk of coin also, fourteen dollars. But alas, nobody has accepted the offer.

I also have spent several hours on the Khan Academy website, trying to learn Algebra from its most basic level. The result is that I'm still bad at Algebra, but I'm now also blind in my left eye from too much time staring at the computer.

I'm not even sure why I need to know it. Let's face it, statistics show more correlation between being attractive and being successful than being intelligent and successful.

I stumble into the bathroom and begin brushing my teeth. After completing the mundane but necessary personal hygiene activities, I head down the stairs to the living room. I used to always eat breakfast at school; in fact it was almost my entire motivation for going there. But that was before the economy forced some serious school budget cuts. Of course, none of the sports teams were negatively affected.

The computer labs however had to downgrade their operating system to Windshield XPP. It does have Oregon Trail so I can't be too angry. Although it doesn't make much sense to me that I can pay for an Indian to get me across the river and still end up drowning.

One side effect is that the cafeteria food seems to have changed into something completely abnormal. Let's just say, the chicken doesn't taste like anything that would be approved by the Food and Drug Administration. Its contents are known only to the three old ladies with hairnets who produce it.

Truth be told, I have no plan to go to school today anyways. I awake at the normal time for school because there is always a possibility my parents could come home from work early. I leave the house every morning as if I was going to school, but that is rarely where I end up.

It's a beautiful day outside and I soon find myself sharing a cup of coffee with Jamie Salmens. Coffee Café is a bit overpriced, but enjoyable since you can sit outside and get a free refill. My budget is pretty low, but it's not every day that Jamie skips school with me. In fact, it's never happened before.

She is sipping a frappe, which seems to be the preferred choice of most high school girls. I, on the other hand, am indulging in what can only be called a post-modern classic, hot chocolate.

Jamie and I have been friends for seemingly an eternity, but that in itself is a bit of an enigma. We really share not a single thing in common other than our enrollment at Dale Bridge High.

Our basis of conversation usually has to do with our current situations in life. She is very optimistic, the yin to my realistic yang. Only she thinks my realism is just a disguised version of negativity.

"Is there a purpose to anything?" I say as Jamie stares back at me in bewilderment.

"What are you talking about?"

"I don't know. I suppose I awoke this morning not on the wrong side of the bed, but the wrong bed altogether."

Jamie leans forward and whispers.

"Are you taking drugs?"

"No, well just Nyquil. Listen, I don't mean to ruin a beautiful day with my esoteric ramblings. How have you been?"

"Great. School has been keeping me busy, but it's worth it."

"I wish I shared your zest for education."

"I watched the Notebook last night."

"Oh, I'm sorry."

"You didn't like it?"

"I didn't like the gender bias. It was clearly made for women."

"Guys like it too."

"Name one."

"Jimmy enjoyed it."

I laugh. "I find that hard to believe."

"He did, I'm telling you."

"Well, that doesn't hold much weight. He's your boyfriend."

"So?"

"He was just telling you what you wanted to hear."

She shakes her head, as if the mere thought of what I said is too silly to consider.

"He hates many things that I like."

"Maybe he purposely does that to throw you off."

"Why would he go to so much trouble?"

"It's simple human psychology really. For example, if I had all the answers to a test, I would still have to make sure that I miss a few. If I got them all right, the teacher would be suspicious."

She sighs. I mock her sigh by taking a deep, overdrawn breath. She in response throws a cherry at my head. Thankfully, I duck and the cherry sails onto the table behind us. I turn and see an old couple has stopped talking as a random cherry with a bit of whip cream attached to it now sits on their table.

"Oops", I say, even though it seems it was Jamie's fault for throwing the cherry initially.

I'm just happy she actually showed up.

Although I'm sure she enjoys the pleasure of my company, I can't presume that hanging out with me was enough to get her away from her books. Maybe she is getting in touch with her seldom used rebellious side.

"The Notebook is one of the most romantic movies of all time."

"Romantic is one word for it. Another would be unrealistic."

"What do you mean?"

"You thought the story of their love bringing back her memory was even remotely possible?"

"It could happen."

"No, that's taking liberties on reality in order to make a love story more exciting. Love has no say with medical conditions."

"Well, I disagree."

"That's because you are a romantic, but you don't have to be jaded like me to see how crazy it is. At the end they fall asleep and die together. Has that ever happened in the history of the human race? I think not."

She sighs again. She has a happy sigh, which this most certainly was not, a tired sigh, and an agitated sigh. Yes, that is the one she has given. She was pretty gung ho at the outset, but suddenly she doesn't seem too thrilled with our class cutting adventure.

Maybe she just isn't used to it. She is after all a straight laced honors student with a bright future in which she'll contribute greatly in some shape or form to the advancement of human society.

Me? I'm just trying to make it to through the day without breaking something. Sure, I want to do something with my life. I'm just not sure what. And I honestly don't know why everybody is in such a big rush to figure it out. My fellow seniors are having mental breakdowns, exhausted and stressed from filling out college applications and then having panic attacks when they don't get accepted. I prefer to play it cool. I'm like a modern day Fonze, just without the cool leather jacket. Oh, and of course without the social acceptance from my peers.

"So this is what you do when you skip school?" She looks at me and then looks at the tables around us. There aren't many people here, and especially no other teenagers. I like that. In its conspicuousness, it's a safe place to be skipping school.

"You should be happy to know that we're here solely in honor of you joining me. My normal class cutting activities are actually far more low-key. "

"Are you going to homecoming?"

Homecoming, just thinking about it makes me feel a bit empty.

"I don't think so."

I look down at the hot chocolate. The taste of something sweet is never enough to sooth the bitter thoughts that fly through my head. In four years of high school, I've missed every single homecoming dance, mostly though consistent self-sabotage. This would be my last chance to go.

"Why didn't we go skating?" Jamie wonders out loud.

Simple, I think to myself. I can't skate. I also can't dance, fix things, or do much of anything that takes a requisite amount of physical skills. Physical activities are for the coordinated, I prefer to watch movies and drink herbal tea.

"Skating is totally out of style."

I'm hoping that sounds reasonable.

"I still enjoy it", she says in passing. Beyond the voice, Jamie is empirically an attractive person. She has long blonde hair, involving brown eyes, and a true sense of fashion. Maybe if we had known each other in a different lifetime, things would be different. As is, it would be safe to say that she and I are firmly entrenched in the friend zone. And that's likely where we belong. We've known each other since the eighth grade. And once you've been friends for that long, there is no turning back.

You're probably thinking that through some oddball chain of events, I'm going to end up with her at the end of my plight. That would be wrong for a couple of reasons. First of all, I don't have a plight. I live a rather uneventful life, the likes of which wouldn't even make the headlines of the poorly run Dale Bridge High Gazette. Yes, my world is concealed like an air tight vacuum, and that's how I prefer it.

Secondly, to even approach her on a romantic level would be taking my rather simple universe, and turning it into a complicated arubex cube. We are friends, and that means by definition, we must never think beyond that. The poor guy who falls for his female friend is destined to a life of agony and solitude. So even though I've admitted I find her attractive, I have to refrain myself from having any interest in her romantically. And it's not so difficult to keep my heart at a distance when our opposite interests are considered.

Academically, we are artists working on different canvases. She puts in an amount of effort into her school work that I just can't comprehend. I'm still trying to figure out why the people who are in charge of high schools have decided that cramming our minds with useless information and routinely testing our short term memory is the best way for us to get an education.

Most importantly, she is in a relationship with the Notebook loving Jimmy Winston. He is the biggest bully in school, and for the life of me I can't figure out what she would ever see in him.

"Have you read the Alchemist?" She asks.

"Yes, it's about the boy who goes to find his personal treasure."

"You know, you read a lot for someone who skips school."

"Yeah, I didn't really like it though. It was too much of a fantasy."

"You don't believe in someone having a personal legend?"

"You mean like destiny or fate? No way. You believe that

stuff?"

Her face lights up. I've struck another positive emotional chord in her.

"Absolutely, destiny is like when a hero saves a princess! And fate is when the villain meets his demise!" She has the type of innocent smile that projects a high sense of idealism.

"Yes, I concede that there is such a thing as fate and destiny in la-la land. But how about we try to practically apply those terms to real life situations? For example, let's look at all of the unemployed people in America. You think it's their fate or destiny to sit on their couch and watch the Home and Garden Channel?"

"Is there something wrong with the Home and Garden channel?"

"No", I admit.

"I feel bad for those people, but not everybody makes the right decisions in life. It doesn't mean they weren't at some point given a chance to take a different path."

"Ok, what about the guy who invented those scooter things in Europe?"

"You mean Tri Scooters?"

"Yes. Last week, the inventor of them was riding one and fell off a cliff. You really think that was the big plan for his life? A watery death at the hands of his own invention?"

"That's tough, but it could have happened to anybody."

"Jamie, where did your whole positive outlook on the world come from?"

She takes just a second to think it over.

"I've always been that way. Why look at the world negatively? You have to make Orange Juice, you know?"

"Yeah, but what if all you have is lemons. You can't possibly make Orange Juice out of lemons, can you?"

She gives no response, electing instead to shake her head.

I sigh. "I don't know. Maybe high school did this to me."

She looks at her watch.

"I think I better get back to school before my next class."

"So I only get you for an hour?"

"Sorry McKay."

I don't know why she calls me by my last name, no one else does.

"Jimmy will be looking for me in Trig."

The big rumor is that Jimmy and his gang are dealing drugs to select members of the faculty. But I don't tell Jamie that because I don't want to upset her.

"So you guys are going to Homecoming?" I ask.

"Absolutely", she says with a cheerful smile. Bless her fairytale believing heart. I imagine she'll feel like Cinderella at the ball.

I should actually tell her about Jimmy's drug scandal anyways. It wouldn't be because I'm jealous. It's just that I only have two friends, so it really does affect my life when one of them disappears into relationship purgatory. And it's only a matter of time before Jimmy two times her.

"Well, if you're going back to school, I guess I'll go home and watch a movie."

"Do you still download them?"

"Yes."

"Isn't that illegal?"

"Technically, yes. But it's just as common as tipping a waitress. Alright maybe not such a staple of society, but it's becoming fairly universal."

"It doesn't seem very ethical."

"It's not an issue of ethics. Downloading movies is the next logical step in the advancement of internet technology. Look at music. Everybody gets songs for free now. Why not get movies for free also?"

"It's breaking the law."

"Hey, you've gone to all those parties that have underage people drinking alcohol, what about that?"

"Did you see me drinking at any of those parties?

"I don't know. I've never been to one."

She laughs. I chuckle a little bit also although I'm secretly wondering why we're laughing at all. My not going to parties doesn't seem too funny.

"Are you going to come to school today?'

I shake my head immediately.

"I don't miss school, and it doesn't miss me."

"What about your grades?

"I don't miss them either."

"You're so anti-establishment."

"That would have made me a rebel in the sixties."

"And a misunderstood outcast in our generation."

"Is that what people think?

"Not me, I know you."

"I like the misunderstood part."

She looks at her watch again.

"Let me know how it goes. I'm going to head back."

"Have fun in school."

Now I realize why she wanted to take separate cars.

"Hey, what do you think happened to Samantha?" Jamie asks.

"What do you mean?'

"You didn't hear? She's missing."

"What?"

"She didn't come home last night."

"How do you know that?"

"It was on Facebook. Her parents are looking for her. Someone saw here at Steak and Bake last night."

"Are the police involved?"

"It has to be forty eight hours before they can report her missing."

"I saw her last night. "

"Where? "

"At Steak and Bake. I was there with my parents."

"Did you talk to her?"

"Yeah, she was looking for a ride home. I offered one, but she said she would just walk."

"That's crazy."

"Maybe she went out of town?"

"But would she go anywhere alone? None of her friends are

missing."

"So than you think something bad happened to her?"

"I hope not. She was going to be homecoming queen."

"She had a one out of four chance."

"Do you think that has something to do with her missing?"?

"Maybe if this were a horror movie."

"I don't like horror movies, they're so nihilistic."

"But they are fun too. Where else can we see people die at the hands of a killer voice mail?"

"Do you think Samantha will turn up?"

"It seems more reasonable than the contrary. I mean this is Dale Bridge. We don't exactly have the reputation of say the Bermuda Triangle. When does anything that bad ever happen around here?"

"I guess you're right."

I sure hope so.

On the way home I look in my rear view mirror and see an old beat up Blue Chevy Nova right behind me. They aren't close enough for me to make out the driver.

It's an otherwise normal thing, except for the fact that they have been behind me since I left the coffee shop. That is suspicious mainly because I have taken an unusual combination of small back roads that allow me to avoid traffic. This Chevy Nova could possibly live in my neighborhood, and it's conceivable that they too have discovered this short cut.

But that seems absurd and highly coincidental.

The more logical scenario is that I'm being followed.

But what have I done to warrant that?

Could it be somebody from the school administration?

That would only make sense if it was the principal from Ferris Bueller's Day Off.

Besides, the school would only be on to me if they had been given a reason to investigate my whereabouts.

Maybe it's the fact that Samantha is missing that has me a bit more paranoid than usual.

I turn onto my street and look in my mirror.

The Chevy Nova keeps driving straight.

Maybe it was just my imagination.

My home life is pretty standard. When my parents get home from work they scream at me to do the dishes, clean my room, and scrape tar off the driveways.

I jog up to my closet sized room and take a seat in front of the keyboard. I'm a proud card carrying member of the YouTube generation. Well, we should have cards. Any fun little video on planet earth at my disposal, how could anyone resist?

I sit at my computer for the next half an hour and watch an old episode of "Freaks and Geeks." I have my e-mail opened up in another window, as well as the program that I use for downloading movies in a third window. The multi-tasking abilities of modern computers are truly something to behold.

I get a text from Kenny around twelve telling me that he's stopping by on his way home from school in order to borrow Madden. It's around than that I notice that Saw 12 has finished downloading.

I click on the file to open it, but instead of the movie, I see an error message pop up.

You have reached the limit on downloading movies.

What the hell? I click on the file one more time and again get the same error message. Guess it's a bad file. It's just than that the house phone rings.

"Hello", I say as I hold the receiver to my ear and chew on Sour Patch Kids.

"Is this Mr. McKay?"

"This is his son."

"I'm contacting you about a very serious matter."

I wonder if this is somebody from the school administration.

"What's going on?" I ask.

"This is Fast Net. We've been monitoring your activity and we've seen that you've been illegally downloading movies."

It's worse than the school administration, it's the cable company.

"How could you possibly know that?"

"We are required to give you a warning before any further action is taken."

"Wow, alright."

"Did you have any questions?"

"Is there any way you can make the internet faster?"

"No."

"Can we have free HBO for a month?"

"No."

"No questions then."

"You have a great day, bye."

I put the phone down.

My downloading movies adventure is over.

Kenny drops by my house a few moments after the call from the cable company.   He is a bit of a computer genius and likewise a complete math wiz. He also is tall, very tall. At 6'2, he stands above most of the teachers at school.

"Do you want to watch Saw 12?" I ask.

"Is that the one in theaters?"

"No, that's Saw 13. Saw 12 is the one that came out six months ago."

"I'll pass. So how is skipping school going?"

"I prefer to call it living life to its fullest."

"But we're graduating in eight months."

"And according to the Mayan calendar, the world may end in two. Why not go out with a bang?"

"Skipping school to hang at a coffee shop doesn't seem like much of a bang. You should come to school and be a real student again."

I chuckle.

"Kenny, you poor soul. You're trapped in a web of school books and barely edible cafeteria food. When will you learn?"

"Didn't you hear about Ryan Buford?"

I'm half paying attention to him and half trying to find a granola bar that I left somewhere near the couch yesterday.

"Eric."

"Yes, sorry. Ryan Buford, starting point guard on the varsity basketball team, what about him?"

"He used to skip school all the time just like you. One day he was at the grocery store with his father. They get in line to pay, and a girl from English class gets in line right behind them."

"Ok."

"So right in front of his father, the girl says 'hey Ryan, how come you haven't been in class?"

"Yikes."

"His father contacts the school, and now he's in trouble from both sides. Suspended from school and grounded at home."

"All because of a coincidence."

"It wasn't a coincidence. It was a misguided philosophy about having fun in life that did him in."

"I'd say the meaning is open to interpretation."

"Did you not understand the moral?"

"Don't go to the grocery store with your dad?"

"I don't think that was it."

"I'm just saying that coincidences happen all the time. Everything that happens to us isn't meant to be a life lesson. Sometimes things go wrong in a very random and meaningless way."

"His luck ran out, so could yours."

"Skipping school is not a matter of luck. Ryan violated the system. He should have known that if your cutting class you don't go anywhere with your parents where a fellow classmate may see you."

"What system?"

"I can email you a PDF version if you'd like."

"That's alright. Are you going to Homecoming?"

"I don't have a date."

"Everybody goes."

"People love a bandwagon."

"A part of you has to want to go to at least one dance before you graduate."

"And what about not having a date?"

"The way I see it, you're a decent looking guy and you can

dance. That's more than enough to get a date."

"I don't think being able to do the Macarena qualifies me as a good dancer. Plus the dance is in three days."

"Sure, but remember there are twenty percent more girls in the senior class than boys."

"So?"

"So just ask a girl who is planning on going with a group of friends."

"She would already be going with her friends."

"But she would much rather have a real date. She knows that's the only way she can have the flowers, limo, a guaranteed dance partner, you know all the traditional stuff that girls love and guys don't pay attention too."

"I don't have money for a limo."

"You can leave that part out."

"I don't know man."

"You can ask out Tracy Hill."

"I would have a better chance at decoding the Matrix and translating it in Spanish."

"What happened to living life to the fullest? You never know until you ask."

"In this case, I know. Look, it's all shoe leather anyways."

"What?"

"It's meaningless, homecoming I mean."

"You really don't want to go?"

I hesitate before speaking. Where is this hesitation coming from?

"I'm so detached from all of it."

"Why don't you try coming to school tomorrow? You can get a vibe for everything. Maybe it will lift your school spirit."

"What are they serving at lunch?"

"Steak and Cheese Stromboli."

"Doesn't that usually taste like chicken?"

"You can get the pizza."

"You mean the, 'it's not delivery or Digourno's, in fact you'll never guess what it is' pizza?"

"That's it."

"I'll think about it. I'm not sure I want to go to Algebra."

"I have Trig and you're complaining about some school house rocks level Algebra?"

"Math is not for everybody my friend."

"What happened to the Algebra for Dummies book I gave you

for your birthday?"

"Probably in my closet next to the Bill Gates biography you bought me last year."

"What else better do you have to do tomorrow?"

"It just so happens that a girl from an online dating site just e-mailed me back. She said it would be cool for us to meet."

"Which online dating site?"

"PlentyofTrout.com"

"You're going on a blind date?"

"It's not a blind date."

"You met her online, what do you call it?"

"I met her online, yes. But, you have to take into account that I've not only read her profile information, I've actually seen her profile picture as well."

"What made you sign up for an online dating site? You see girls at school every day."

"Yes, but that would imply that I actually go to class."

"But you really think you're going to meet a quality girl online?"

"You never know what's just around the river band."

"What?"

"Oh sorry, I was watching Pocahontas last night.

"I'm not even going to ask why."

"Well, if this date works out maybe I'll ask her to homecoming."

I walk Kenny out to the front porch.

As he's leaving, I see it across the street.

The blue Chevy Nova.

I still can't make out the driver.

The engine roars up and the Nova drives off suddenly.

I close my front door and lock it.

A few minutes later find I find myself working on an experimental soup. It's chicken noodle with slabs of turkey and honey mustard thrown in. That may sound disgusting in theory, but in practice some of the best food dishes have been known to materialize from throwing random ingredients together. At least, that's what the Italian guy on the Food Network says. For me, it's a hit or miss affair. My Frosted Flakes with Grapes from yesterday hadn't been great. But I am fairly hopeful about what I'm calling my Turkey and Chicken Noodle Honey Mustard Surprise.

As I wait for the soup to finish, I think back to where I've gone wrong in high school. The world of high school that was presented to me through television and movies back when I was a kid turned out to be a myth. They would always show cool characters with nice cars with the self-confidence of thirty year olds. They would delegate the shy, insecure guy to a supporting role when in fact the majority of high school students are the insecure person who isn't quite comfortable in their own skin.

It got bad pretty fast. But, I didn't start skipping every day until this, my senior year. I always thought the school would call my house. They never have. I suppose they really just expect the parents to call in. With both my parents and the school assuming I'm in class, it's actually pretty hard to get caught.

I should be content to continue this routine and move on with my life in June. But recently, thoughts of attending Homecoming have begun to creep into my head. I'm not sure why.

It would all be better if I had a job. I would almost certainly have a better social life since if you have more money you can buy better clothes and accessories and project a better public image to the mass sheep of high school students.

Yes, all the cool kids wear designer clothing and have necklaces and chains that would make Mr. T proud. They also have money to go out and do fun stuff. My weekends consist of whatever is in my fridge combined with whatever I'm watching on television. That would maybe be acceptable if it wasn't what I already do on weekday nights.

Yes, I'm a home body, somewhat by choice. Would I go out on the weekends if I had money to do so? Who knows if the grass is greener at the mall? I can't help but notice that the things I do for fun are the same things my parents do for fun. The problem there is that they are fifty and I am seventeen. My life should be an exciting rollercoaster ride, not a walk down the street to Grandma's house.

"Why does my life have to be this way?" I say out loud.

I stir my soup a bit, trying to find the right combination of thickness and liquidness.

"SAVE THEM!"

I stop stirring my soup. That's peculiar. I could have sworn I just heard a loud voice saying the words 'save them.'

"SAVE THEM!"

Ok, I know I heard it that time.

Wait, what the hell? It's a distant, fading voice. Strange, I know nobody is home. I do leave the television on in my room sometimes, but that wouldn't be loud enough for me to hear it all the way downstairs in the kitchen.

The voice had a whispering tone. I turn the stove off and listen closer.

I wait for anything, but suddenly silence is golden.

I had thought it to be a girl's voice. Could it have been a house noise?

House noises are easy to explain, like when the fridge rumbles or the stairs creak. The movie Paranormal Activity made millions of dollars based on people's fear of house noises. But a house noise would never be so specific as to say 'save them.'

Yes, it was a voice alright. And that makes the hairs on my arm rise in unison.

I put my soup on hold and slowly walk around the house searching for the origins and the whereabouts of 'the female voice'. The problem is that I'm not hearing it anymore. It had happened twice and then the voice had vanished into whatever form of air it had come from.

I must admit, this is actually incident number two. Incident number one happened yesterday, and it's the reason why this incident today is far more troubling. You see, one incident typically isn't enough to assume supernatural activity. Hearing a voice could have been a figment of my imagination, or it could have spoken to my own personal lack of insanity. But I consider myself to be pretty sane.

I was in my bathroom yesterday turning the water on when I

remembered I had left my towel back in my bedroom. I walked out of the bathroom and to my towel which as I had suspected was lying on my bed. I than walked back to the bathroom where I discovered the door had been closed. And not just closed, it was locked!

"Hey, who locked the door?" I said out loud. I looked down and saw a little bit of steam begin to leak out from under the door. I'm a big fan of extremely hot showers in the morning. The hot water only runs for a few minutes before it runs out and turns icy cold. That means all my hot water was going to waste!

Stupidly, I knocked on the door. If there was somebody in there, it was unlikely they were going to hear somebody knocking and actually open the door. My stupid actions could somewhat have been attributed to my lack of a morning shower to snap me out of my normal morning funk.

"If anyone is in there, you better get out before I come in!"

A silly threat, but I did remember that I had a spare key for this bathroom in the kitchen drawer.

I ran downstairs and found the key located just where I thought it would be.

"Yes!"

I walked back up the stairs and right back to the bathroom door.

The key went right in but as I put my hand the door it opened by itself without me having to turn the key. So now it was somehow unlocked.

I cautiously pushed the bathroom door open and saw that the shower was still on.

Maybe the steam pushed the door shut?

No, that doesn't make sense. Steam can't push doors. And it certainly can't lock them.

Everything in the bathroom was how I had left it except for one important thing.

The shower door had somehow slid open.

I remembered lucidly that I had closed that shower door before leaving the bathroom.

Creepy.

Even worse, I now had to take my morning shower in cold water.

Somebody or something had used up my hot water.

That was yesterday.

Today, Samantha is missing, and a voice is telling me to save them.

Save who?

The next morning, I awake with the intention of heading to Waffles Galore for breakfast. My shower goes off without a hitch. As usual, I shave even though I lack any amount of facial hair that would justify it. I dress in my room with the comfort of hearing no strange voices and encountering no locked doors. Everything has returned to normal.

I'm soon in the dining room, ready to leave the house and go about my normal schedule. I just have to grab my car keys from my computer desk in my room. I whistle peacefully as I make my way up the stairs.

I grab the car keys off my desk.

I notice my computer monitor is on, even though I had shut it off earlier.

"What is this?" I say out loud.

On the computer screen, Microsoft Word is opened up.

It is an otherwise blank document except for the big message that is on the screen.

SAVE THEM!

Strike three.

Could it be a virus on my computer? I've never heard of a virus that does this.

I have to get out of here.

But, I'm clearly not crazy in thinking that something is terribly wrong at my house.

Am I?

5

My house is being haunted by some type of spirit. And it likely yearns to take over my room and eradicate my body like coffee beans in an Espresso machine.

That is the best conclusion I can come too.

I step out of my car and walk to the front door of Waffles Galore where I pause and look down.

The word 'WHY' has been spray-painted on the curb in big black letters.

There is something else spray-painted on the wall next to the door.

'WHY NOT?"

Touché. I appreciate that the vandal took the time to properly add a question mark.

I walk through the double doors and head toward the register.

To my dismay, I notice that Waffles Galore is unusually crowded for a Tuesday afternoon.

This place usually invites an older selection of customers, and today is no different. I see many senior citizen types, probably enjoying retirement. I've always wondered if I would get happier with age. So far I've gotten progressively more miserable.

I'm near the register when I spot a girl who looks to be my age sitting in a booth in the back. I notice her suddenly because I believe she is staring at me.

Half of her is hidden in the shadows, but at least one half seems to be eying me in intended secrecy. But she doesn't look away when she sees me staring at her. Well, maybe not intended secrecy after all.

I should look away right now but my gaze doesn't falter.

I'm way past the regular acceptable time of staring at somebody.

She leans forward, coming out of the shadows.

She is a cute girl. That's an initial impression that changes almost immediately. She is just sort of cute actually.

A cup of coffee sits in her hands, and a paperback copy of Gone with the Wind.

She is in high school. I know this because she has a backpack on the table next to her purse. She could be in college, but the university is on the other side of town.

The coffee stands out. Although I'm a coffee loving son of a gun, most people my age drink Red Bull.

Her choice of literature is also a surprise. Margaret Mitchell's civil war epic that also spawned a classic film. I've never seen it, but I've read about it on Wikipedia. Maybe she is reading it for a class.

There is something else about her. It's on the tip of my mind.

Have I seen her before? Maybe at school?

I look towards the entrance way where a host of people walk in.

"Are you alright?"

I turn behind me and see an older gentleman who is also waiting in line.

"Yes sir", I say politely.

He takes a step forward and raises his eyebrow.

"You look a bit unhappy that's all."

My parents do say I should smile more often.

But why smile if I'm not happy? That would contradict my indifference.

"I'm just really hungry."

I almost forget to respond to him, something I tend to do quite often. My inner thoughts and reality are like two parallel universes fighting for the same space and time. Maybe if I went to school more often I would have the technical knowledge to elaborate, but I don't suppose they would teach us about parallel universes anyways.

He stares for a moment and then eases back.

"Don't we all. My son is getting married next week. I really thought he had a few years left."

I stay quiet.

"The cost of this wedding is driving me crazy."

It's not that I don't care. It's just that I can't relate to his problem. I can relate to the idea of having a problem, but not specifically his. My world is full of dances, cliques, and pointless electives. He lives in a world of car payments, mortgages, and marriages. It would be hard for either of us to relate.

To be fair, I do pay my monthly cell phone bill, but that's with a weekly allowance that I get from my parents. And I don't even get that unless I mow the lawn every two weeks.

"And the in-laws, they are a problem to themselves."

One of the disadvantages to public eating is this. A friendly man who is going to tell me his story whether I want to hear it or not.

"Good luck with that", I say as I walk to the register to make my order.

"I'll take a steak and egg burrito."

The cashier is an older woman with pearly white teeth.

"We don't serve that anymore."

"What? I just ordered it two days ago."

"That was its last day."

"Well, I wasn't expecting that."

"Would you like something else?"

"Yeah, just need a moment."

I'm so in love with the steak and egg burrito that I haven't tried much of anything else here.

"Can I have the Waffle and Cheese burrito?"

"Sure."

I'm a bit skeptical. Waffles and Cheese don't seem to fit together at all.

"Are you off from school today?"

It's the marriage guy; still initiating conversation with me after I assumed it was over.

"You could say that."

He smiles.

"High school, now that was the greatest time of my life."

I nod and walk over to the left of the counter where I await my food.

The girl in the back seems to be into her book now.

I'm looking at a book of my own, the Chocolate War. It's about a counsel of students who run a school and make other students do unethical missions for them. It has an underlying theme of being accepted by your peers or being beaten to a bloody pulp. Now that sounds like high school.

My mind however is still preoccupied with the girl.

I've been gathering mental notes about her with every glance. She has a thin face and medium sized dark hair. There is one unusual thing about her choice of clothing. A light jacket even though it's warm outside.

It hits me just then. I know where I've seen her before.

She was here at this exact same time two days ago. Of course!

Why didn't she register on my radar then? She was sitting in a booth on the opposite site of where she's sitting now, but she wasn't staring at me than. Not the way she is today.

I quickly form two possible reasons for her being here. She could just love Waffles Galore. That seems like a decent coincidence. The other possibility is that she is here because of me.

Even if she's just here to eat, she is violating the system. The larger than expected populace of students skipping school on a regular basis follow a certain system that maybe has been in place since the beginning of time. It can't be found in the school's code of behavior and it is not really talked about openly, but it's universally known amongst class cutters.

The key ingredient of the system is to go to different places every week. Last week for example I went to Hash Brown Heaven, and this week it's been Waffles Galore. Everybody has their own patterns and schedules, but they normally fall within the rules of the system, and because of that it's rare for two people to randomly cross paths at the same place in the same week.

I have to find out why she's here.

"I've seen you before."

I stand next to her booth. She slightly lowers her book and raises her eyes. She doesn't look surprised to see me.

"That's nice."

"You were here two days ago."

"I know that, thank you."

I realize something else just then.

"And you were at Steak and Bake the other night also. You're in the math club!"

"Are you writing my biography?"

"No, but listen I really think for us to make this work we should stick to the system."

"You have cheese on your shirt."

I look down. Damn. I wipe the cheese off.

"About the System."

"What system is that?"

"You know the system."

"Actually I don't."

"You're skipping class, right?"

"I enjoy the coffee."

"The hot chocolate is better."

"So what's the problem?"

"Simple. It's not safe for two class cutters to be seen at the same place. If somebody from the school sees us here they may mention it to somebody important. And then this whole cutting class adventure may fall under the microscope of the administration, in which we'd be doomed."

She takes a sip of the coffee.

"So what do you suggest we do about it?"

"It won't take much for us to restore order to our universe. We just need you go to a different place tomorrow."

"But I like the coffee here."

"They have great coffee at Starbucks."

"No they don't."

"Well maybe not. How about a compromise? I'll come here in the morning, and you come in the afternoon."

"I only drink coffee in the morning."

"Do you mind if I take a seat?"

She shrugs, so I sit down.

"Do you skip every day?" I ask.

"Just when I'm in the mood for coffee."

"Coffee seems to be an important part of your life."

"Not really."

"I have to ask, what is with the light jacket?"

She puts her hands on her jacket and looks at it before looking back at me. Her green eyes seem powerful enough to cast a spell.

"Do you think it's too warm outside?"

"Some would say so."

"Some would be wrong."

"Some are usually wrong, but a light jacket in warm weather seems universally wrong."

"Let's forget about my jacket."

"Sure. I noticed you have green eyes."

"What about them?"

"They're sort of interesting."

"Sort of?"

"I don't deal in absolutes."

"Interesting isn't much of a compliment."

"Right. Look, the bottom line is I don't want either of us to get into trouble. Why don't I just go to Denny's from now on?"

I stand from the table, somewhat satisfied. It was just a mutual coffee loving coincidence that brought us here, nothing more. I can go back to my normally scheduled programming.

"You shouldn't be so quick to settle, Eric."

Ok, so maybe there is more than meets the coffee.

"You know my name?"

"Yes."

"I'm not very popular."

"Take a seat."

I sit back down. Now her eyes seem suddenly focused.

"We made eye contact fifteen minutes ago, so you know I was looking at you. There is no reason to be alarmed, or excited for that matter."

"Excited?"

"You are a high school boy."

"I'm eighteen next month."

"But you look like a boy."

"Guess I'll start doing push-ups every night before bed."

"We don't have much time Eric."

"Do you have to get back to school?"

"No. It isn't safe there."

"Are they on the lookout for class cutters?"

"That's not what I mean."

She looks out of the glass window behind her before speaking again.

"I'd like to be up front with you. But I'm not sure how you're going to take it."

"I'm very open-minded."

She nods.

"Ok, here goes. Dale Bridge is in serious danger. And we need your help to save it."

I immediately erupt with laughter. It's a natural reflex of sorts. I calm down a little when I see she hasn't cracked a smile.

"Do you have a red pill and a blue pill that you want me to choose from?"

"I'm sure you're used to taking medication. But no, I don't have any pills."

"Is this a senior prank? I thought you just enjoyed the coffee here."

"I do. But there are more important things going on."

I'm at a loss for words. I decide to bring this conversation down to earth.

"Can I have your name?"

She hesitates.

"It's not important."

"It is for me."

"Ok. I'm Kelly."

"That wasn't so hard right?"

"No", she says seriously.

"Alright, let me think about this. Alright, let's say for a second the town is in danger. What do you need me for? I'm a class cutter with absolutely zero extra-curricular activities on my high school resume."

"It's complicated."

"Are you sure you're in high school?"

"Have you ever heard of the whole need to know basis thing?"

"Sure, it's a well-established government cliché."

She leans forward.

"I can't explain right now, but we need your help. "

"You don't even know me, how could you need my help?"

"I do know you."

"Hey, you may have watched me eat a Waffle and Cheese Burrito, but that hardly qualifies you as an Erick McKay expert."

"You talk a lot for an introvert."

"What makes you think I'm an introvert?"

"Aren't you?"

"Well I hardly think it matters, but yeah."

"It doesn't matter, your right. All that matters is that you help us."

"No."

"What?"

"That's my answer."

She looks annoyed.

"I haven't given you any details yet."

"The details will only add onto my no."

"I thought you didn't deal in absolutes?"

"So I'm a seventeen year old walking contradiction. I at least know the difference between right and wrong. And this sounds both wrong and incredibly risky. I'm graduating in eight months."

"And yet you're openly skipping school. That really makes sense."

"As long as certain people follow the system I should be fine."

Her eyes narrow in concentration as she puts her hand on mine.

"Listen, I don't mean to invade your small world where skipping high school has a system, but you need a reality check. Your life is easy, simple even. Your world can come crashing down on you any second now. And your negative outlook will do nothing to save you then."

She leans back and takes another sip of the coffee.

"I like that thing you did with your hand, putting it on mine."

She sighs. "This is a waste of time."

"Listen, I am open minded about this. There have been weird things going on lately, especially at my house."

"Like what?"

"You wouldn't believe me."

"Like you didn't believe me a moment ago?"

"I'm still not sure I do. I mean, really, who are you?"

"I told you."

"Yes, but it's pretty obvious you're not the typical high school girl who is thinking about homecoming. If you want me to take this all seriously I'm going to need some more information."

She raises an eyebrow at my mention of homecoming.

"Can you get me another coffee?" She asks.

"What?"

"Another coffee, I would like one."

"We just met and you want me to buy you something?"

She pulls out some change.

"I'm sorry. I don't want to be a financial burden. Here is the eighty five cents for the coffee."

"Thanks."

I stand from the table and walk away. When I return with the coffee a moment later, she is standing with the book in her hand.

"I have to go."

I hand her the coffee.

"Listen, maybe I should get your number in case I have to contact you."

"That won't be necessary."

I can't help but feel a little bit rejected.

"Should I go to Denny's tomorrow?"

"It doesn't matter."

She starts to walk away but turns back towards me.

"If I were you, I wouldn't go back to school."

She's out the door before I can respond.

6

Kelly. Why didn't I get her last name? I could have looked her up on Facebook.

It all seemed like a joke, and yet she seemed extremely serious when saying that she needed my help.

I try to avoid my house as long as possible that day. But

eventually, I have to go home and get ready for my blind date.

Online dating has a horrible stigma attached to it. It's looked at as a desperate act by a hopeless person who can't find a date in real life.

But if over three million people in the country do it, how bad can it be? I'm doing it because I'm frustrated with the selection of women who go to Dale Bridge High. They are for the most part materialistic and vain. I just want a girl who cares about my personality and my intellect.

Alright, so maybe I'm looking for a pot of gold that doesn't exist. Girls my age at least seem to be more one track minded. The guys are no different. Attraction and popularity combine to make the ultimate screening process in the high school dating world.

The beauty of online dating is that you already know the persons interest by looking at their profile. The girl I'm on the way to meet right now is an avid Stephen King reader and likes to go to poetry readings where she like me drinks a mug of coffee with splenda not sugar. A perfect match!

Meanwhile, asking a girl out in high school is like going to the dentist to have my teeth pulled. It comes with far too much pressure attached to it. I have to walk up to the girl when she doesn't look busy, bore her with irrelevant small talk, and then put a huge amount of power in her hands by asking her out.

If she says no, everybody knows about it the next day! Suddenly you're the guy who got rejected. You're the guy who wasn't good enough to take that girl out. Now you're at even more of a disadvantage when you want to ask another girl out, because you better believe she's going to be well aware of your past failures.

I walk into Yogurt for Yuppies at exactly eight and see a blonde haired girl sitting near the back. That can't be the girl I'm looking for, my girl is a brunette. But, this girl waves me over so I walk back to where she's sitting. As I approach, I see that she's eating what looks to be a cup of mint chocolate chip yogurt.

"You're not Courtney, are you?"

She smiles. Not a bad smile.

"Yes!! You must be Jason!"

"It's Eric, actually. I thought you had dark hair?"

"Oh I did, but a few weeks ago I decided to try to something different. Please, sit down."

An auspicious beginning, I think to myself as I take a seat.

"I hope you don't mind but I ordered already", she says.

"That's fine. I actually had a big lunch. So you're a big Stephen King fan?"

"Yeah I am."

"I love the book IT. You know, with the crazy clown? That was a classic. What's your favorite book of his?"

She takes a moment to decide. She must really love his books.

"Night of the Living Dummy."

"Oh, ok."

I scan my memory for some recollection of a Stephen Book with that name. Damn, why does that sound so much like an R.L Stine Goosebumps book? I decide to change the subject.

"You know, it's a big relief to see you here. I thought I might get stood up."

"Really?"

"Yeah, I mean a friend of mine is really skeptical about this whole online dating thing. But I told him that I was open minded and that I would give it a chance. Have you done this kind of thing before?"

"Yes."

"Have you met anybody special?"

That's a stupid question, I think to myself. If she had met somebody special, she wouldn't't' be here meeting me.

She shakes her head.

"Not really."

"I imagine the whole online dating thing is pretty hit or miss, but

I'm ok with that."

"Yeah, I try to stay positive. I've done it five times now; you just never know when you may meet the one."

"Five times huh? So I'm number six." I mean to say more but nothing else comes out.

"This yogurt is really good. Are you sure you don't want some?"

Five failed dates. Wow. Failing on five dates is enough evidence to suggest that she's a big part of the problem.

"I'm ok, thanks. So, I remember in your profile you said you're going to college out of state next year?"

"Well actually, I am going to another state next year, but not for college. I'm going to California to become an actress."

Coincidentally, I read on Google yesterday that seventy percent of women who move to California to become actresses end up as waitresses. I decide to keep that fun fact to myself.

"Really? That's great! So instead of going to college you're going to follow your dreams. That's super pro-active."

"Actually, I already graduated from college."

"You did?"

She takes a bite out of her yogurt.

"Yes I graduated a few years ago."

"Wait, exactly how old are you?"

She smiles, showing a mouth full of green yogurt as she tries to speak.

"26."

"What??? Your profile said you were seventeen!"

"I haven't updated all of my information."

"In nine years??"

"Look, I'm sorry if you have a problem with me being a little older. I liked your profile and thought we would get along well. I'm sorry that I lied to you."

She looks down. I feel bad. Why am I being so immature? There is nothing truly wrong with her being older. I'm seventeen years old, basically an adult. This would be a bit awkward if I was a year or two younger, but I should be able to handle this.

"It's alright", I say finally. "It's not what I expected, but I can handle this. Your right, we're two adults. We should be able to have fun despite the age difference. You know what? I'll have a yogurt!"

"I'm glad you're being mature about this."

Moments later......

"Eric, you've been quiet for a few minutes. Is something wrong?"

Yes, I hate my life and want to die!

"I'm fine, just a little light headed from the yogurt I guess."

She's so old! My great maturity lasted only about two minutes. When she started talking about how she had gotten married and divorced, I suddenly felt a bit out of my element. What am I still doing here?

I finish up my yogurt and start doing a fake yawn.

"Are you tired?" She asks.

"A little bit."

"My mom says that sleep is the cousin of death."

"That's a bit strange."

"Yeah, you know what else is strange?"

"What?"

"Weird messages on Microsoft Word."

I look at her and see a weird looking smile cross her face.

"Excuse me?"

"You got a message earlier today, didn't you?"

What is going on?

"I don't' know what you're talking about."

"Do you want to see something neat?"

Suddenly I see a red liquid start to pour from her nostrils.

I back my chair up.

"Your nose!"

She giggles.

And then the same red liquid starts pouring down from her eyes.

"Oh my God, is that blood?"

"I'm so glad we met!" She says.

And then an overflow of blood starts gushing from her mouth onto the table.

I'm going to be sick!

I stand from the table.

"Look, I have to go. I actually have some homework I have to finish. I have your number, maybe we can do this again some time."

I quickly make my way towards the exit when a waiter stops me.

"Hey buddy, whose going to pay for the yogurt?"

"Just give the bill to that girl sitting at my table."

The waiter looks at me like I'm crazy.

"What are you talking about?" He says.

I turn and in horror see exactly why he is looking at me like that.

There is no girl at the table.

"She was just there!"

The waiter scratches his head.

"There was no girl at the table sir."

I look closely and see no traces of blood anywhere on the table.

I search my pockets and pull a five dollar bill out.

"Keep the change." I hand him the money and run out the door.

7

I decide not to tell anybody about the weird stuff that's been happening to me. I imagine that nobody would believe me without some form of visual evidence. But there was no blood on the table, and even that horrible message on Microsoft Word had been deleted when I had gotten home that day. So whatever is haunting me, I'm on my own until I can present some solid proof.

I sleep restlessly that night. There is a part of me that keeps expecting blood to start pouring from my ceiling onto my forehead.

I try to think all night for a reasonable explanation of what happened on my blind date. I hope I'm not losing my mind.

I have second thoughts about going to school the next day, but truth be told I've already spent all my money for the week. In fact, I had to borrow gas money from my mom last night.

I'm seventy five minutes late to school. It's not that big of deal other than the fact that I promised myself that I was turning over a new leaf and beginning a new era. Skipping school hasn't been working out for me as of late.

I'm driving an old Honda Civic with no air condition, no gas cap, and a rear left door that won't open. When we bought the car last year my parents told me that other kids would like it. It was all about quality, substance over style they had said. But of course they don't go to high school so how could they know.

The Dale Bridge High parking lot is about seven spaces short, so it always comes down to who shows up on time. Since I'm late I'm parking in a reserve parking spot near the football field.

I walk quickly through the parking lot so as not to be seen coming in late.

I enter through the main doors just as first period is letting out. You don't get much of a break in between classes. Six minutes is hardly enough time to go to your locker, use the bathroom, and then throw in whatever socializing you do.

The school has two floors, with only one elevator located at the end of the main hall. And right next to the elevator is the only staircase. And next to the staircase is a vending machine that always holds a line at the beginning of the day. Sure they have a vending machine upstairs, but that's a Coca Cola machine, and everybody in this school seems to love Mountain Dew. I know because any time I try to do the dew, it's sold out and the machine instead spits out a Diet Pepsi, which I immediately throw in the garbage.

I take only a few steps before walking into Dan Fundell.

"Dan, how are you?"

"Winning bro, winning."

"Glad to hear it. Hey when is the next math club meeting?"

"Today bro, after school."

"Oh ok. Well I have to go."

"Be careful man, they're after us!"

"Who?"

"The establishment! They killed the economy, and now they're coming for us!"

"What do you mean the establishment?"

"Nobody knows they're real name!"

"And they're after high school kids?"

"It's the back way in. Preying on the hearts and minds of clueless teenagers, it's sadistic and completely brilliant!"

"Clueless, right."

I start to walk away but Dan stops me.

"Where are you going?"

"To class?"

"That's where they get you man!"

"I'll be careful, thanks."

As I look down the halls, it occurs to me that everybody seems to have some type of group they walk with. I suspect that it's mostly just for show. They may have three hundred friends on Facebook, but that's not an accurate account of how many people they actually talk too.

It takes me forty seconds to make it to my Chemistry class. I'm not looking forward to it. I know about as much about chemistry as I do about boat insurance.

Once everybody is seated and the lecture begins, I zone out.

My usual daydream involves being on a tropical island. The twist is that it's a tropical island that serves coffee instead of smoothies.

Every once in a while I dream about being chased by a Leprechaun, but I think that just depends on what I eat in the morning.

I look to the front of the class and see Tracy talking with one of her friends, maybe about me, probably not. My crush on her began last year. I didn't miss class back then, so I was there in Drama on that first day sitting in the second row making a paper airplane when she took a seat in the chair directly ahead of me. I looked up at her, and the song 'Dreaming of You' by Selena started to play repeatedly in my head. They weren't real feelings though. They were of the superficial variety. In a way, dating her would be like having the newest version of the IPad. And that's pretty impressive for me when you consider I don't even have the oldest version of the IPad.

My chemistry teacher lectures on for about an hour, stopping briefly every once in a while to point at the periodic table that's drawn up on the chalk board. I look around at the rest of the class and see everybody staring ahead blankly. I guess everybody is daydreaming today.

An alarm goes off. My chemistry teacher uses it so she knows when to wrap up her lecture. The students use it as a way to wake up from their deep sleep.

As I walk out, I notice the cheerleaders' right in front of the entrance way to the school gym. They seem chilled and mellow as they lean against a few lockers. They are usually jumping up and down, practicing a cheer right there in the hallway.

Patty Cellars, the head cheerleader, once gave me what she called a popularity test. We were at the time sitting next to each other in eleventh grade English.

"Where did it come from?" I asked.

"We thought of it at practice", she answered.

It made sense at the time, popular people coming up with a test to measure themselves.

"That's very interesting", I said as I looked back at the paper I was working on.

"Do you want to take the test?" She asked. "I need to try it out on somebody".

I put my pen in my ear and turned to her. "Ask away."

"Super", she clapped as she pulled out a neatly folded piece of paper and straightened it out.

"Alright", she began. "Number one, do you like Lord of the Rings?"

"Yes."

"Number two; do you currently have a girlfriend?"

"No".

"Fantastic!"

"Really?"

"That's it, we're done."

She folded the paper neatly and placed it back into her purse.

"Oh ok, so how did I do?"

"Well, according to my results, you measured out as immensely unpopular."

"Just two questions? Wow. Hey, can I ask you a question Patty?"

"Sure."

"What do you want to be when you grow up?"

She chews on that for a brief second.

"I want to be a Kardashian!"

"Oh. But that's not really an occupation."

"What do you mean?"

"Never mind."

She turned around and prepared to give the test to some other poor guy.

She had dated two guys from the football team, so I guess you could say she was already on her way to being a Kardashian.

The athletes don't stay too far away from the cheerleaders, since most of them actually date one. I would like to call them jocks, but the truth is a few of them have become members of the school academic team. They are at the very least smart enough to date the cheerleaders, which ensures popularity for them and negates the fact that many of them are actually quite terrible at the sport they play.

The football team last year had been an abomination to school sports, sporting a 0-15 record. People were crying after they lost the homecoming game by forty five points to their biggest rivals, Forest Green. They haven't been any better this year. I see Jimmy Winston standing with them and he surprisingly nods at me. Even though he dates Jamie, Jimmy normally acts like he doesn't know me.

I walk pass them and into Algebra.

Did I mention I hate Algebra? I hate it worse than Biff from Back to the Future hates manure.

My GPA would be so much better if you simply took out the math classes that I have failed.

Miss Olsen walks in and stands at the front of the class. She's a young lady fresh out of college, entering the lovely world of underpaid teaching.

She talks for a few minutes, something about order of operations. I'm spacing out, thoughts of a random CSI episode come to mind, and did I close the garage door this morning when I left?

When I zone back in, I see five equations on the board, which can only mean one thing.

"Alright class, I'm going to pick five of you to come up here and solve the equations on the board."

I sink down in my chair, trying to be invisible. I figure theirs a good chance of me not being called since its five equations verses twenty four people in the class.

"Eric, would you like to do the first problem?"

How does that happen?

"Well", I start to say.

I must think quickly.

The problem is that the equations on the board are so beyond my level that the only possible outcome I can imagine would be getting laughed at by my classmates and having ham and egg croissants thrown at me.

It's just than that the school's guidance counselor; Mr. Edwards walks into the room.

He talks to Miss Olsen for a second who then motions towards me.

"Eric, Mr. Edwards would like to see you in his office immediately."

Saved.

I think.

Mr. Edwards and I have never gotten along. We haven't had any real problems, but I used to always try to make jokes around him, and he would never laugh. So now I'm pretty serious when I talk to him, which only happens with scheduled appointments. Usually if he randomly comes to class to get someone, it's bad news.

He looks agitated, as if his pet fish has just died.

"Do you know why I've called you here Mr. Mckay?"

"Am I getting some type of award?"

"No, actually we have a problem, Mr. McKay."

"Every problem has a solution. That's what my Chemistry teacher says."

"Yes well this is very serious Mr. McKay."

"You can call me Eric."

"I'm just giving you the same respect that I would expect to be reciprocated."

"I have no problem calling you Mr. Edwards, But I guess as a student, calling me by my last name seems weird."

"Maybe you're not old enough to appreciate being called Mr."

"I guess I just associate it with authority figures."

"I assure you that it's a common term that adults in the professional world adhere too."

"I guess I'll find out when I'm in the real world."

"Well, that kind of gets to the heart of why we're here."

"It does?"

"Yes. We know you were skipping class yesterday."

"How do you know that?"

"We checked in your first period class and saw you were missing. Nobody from your family called us, so we could only come to one conclusion."

This is ok. This will only be bad if they investigated my attendance beyond yesterday.

"It made us curious, so we started talking to a few of your other teachers."

I'm done for.

"As it turns out, you've been missing class quite frequently this year."

It's difficult to claim innocence when being so obviously guilty.

"So what does this mean?"

"I don't know if you've taken a look at your grades as of late."

"Of course I have sir."

"You're failing two classes so far this semester.

"But I'm only taking two classes this semester."

"Yes, I know."

No way to hide the worry from my face now.

"Do you know what happens if you continue your current course?"

I don't respond.

"You wouldn't graduate. You would sit out most senior activities. And you would have to go to summer school to get your degree."

I have to handle this calmly, be cool under pressure.

"Nooooo!!!!!"

I find myself screaming like Darth Vader when he finds out that Padme is dead.

"I'm afraid it's true."

"Can we not tell my parents about this?"

"I'm afraid we have to tell them."

"But it would help out me a great deal if we could just let me solve this on my own."

"Eric, we are going to place you on academic probation."

"What about my parents?"

"If you can show progress over the next few weeks, I won't tell them."

What a relief.

"Thank you."

"There are some things you should know. If you miss class again, you will be suspended. And any work you miss while being suspended, you won't be able to make up. You must turn in all your assignments on time, or you violate the probation and you will be suspended. You're going to have to do well in your classes for these final months. There is no way around it."

"I can do it."

"We're prepared to help you do just that."

"Your encouragement means a lot. Thanks."

"No Eric, I mean you've been signed up for the math club."

"Really?"

"I talked to them and they said they would be happy to have you.

They said for you to be at the meeting today at 1.30."

"I can do that."

8

I walk out of Mr. Edward's office and for some reason run right into Jimmy Winston and the J-Gang. Jimmy has a smug look on his face, the kind of look that says he's a king and I'm a peasant in his palace. It's not all together false. He's a football prodigy, and I'm a slacker who's now on academic probation.

The J-gang is a collection of ruthless boneheads who stick to Jimmy like bubble gum under a desk. Back when Jimmy was a freshman, he had recruited them to watch his back and intimidate the common folk. As a result, Jimmy is untouchable. He has the popularity and the power. Yes, I am incredibly bitter and jealous.

"Eric McKay, how have you been guy?"

His three buddies laugh at the word guy. It's that nervous laughter that people make when something is not funny enough to naturally laugh but they still feel forced too.

"I've been absolutely copasetic."

"You were coming from Mr. Edward's office?"

"He wanted to tell me that if I keep working hard, I'll be in the running for Valedictorian."

"I never knew you were such a scholar."

"It was a rough road, but all the credit goes to my hero, Kernel Sanders."

"That's your role model?"

"Sure. He created the first KFC with a social security check when he was already in retirement."

"What about Mark Zuckerberg? He created Facebook."

"He's absolutely furthered the demise of the youth."

"You're a funny guy Eric. But all of those other guys had something to offer. You can't throw a ninety yard pass, what do you bring to the table?"

"I can paint with all the colors of the wind."

"What?"

"I don't know. So, how is football going?"

"We're doing great. You should have tried out for the team."

I'm not sure if he's being serious or just condescending. Truthfully, I'm not sure why he's even talking to me. He would usually just as soon walk by me than say anything. And there was that nod he gave me earlier. Something is amiss here.

"I have a degenerative condition in my knee. It's a great thought though."

"This guy", Jimmy says looking at his buddies with a smirk. "He gets me every time."

Suddenly, I speak in bold fashion when I probably should just stay silent.

"Hey Jimmy, are you and Jamie going to Homecoming?"

I study his face. He seems surprised by my question, but not angry. Good, that's the reaction I was hoping for.

"Yeah we are", he says simply.

"You know, Jamie is one of my oldest friends."

I now see a subtle hint of annoyance in Jimmy's eyes. Have I perturbed the king?

"You have a thing for Jamie?"

"Not at all", I stammer, nervous only because he has his three buddies with him. Now, I wouldn't expect them to harm me on school property. But, they have been known to jump people outside of school.

"We are absolutely just friends."

"If you do, that's a problem."

"Seems fair, I mean she is your girlfriend."

"Are you going to Homecoming?"

"I'm washing my hair that night actually."

One of the members of the J-gang suddenly speaks up.

"That's too bad. Actually, the event should be only for cool people anyways."

He had insulted me so casually that I almost didn't realize it was an insult.

"Yes", I answer. "It would also weed out most of the intellect as well."

Now there is full blown annoyance showing on Jimmy's face. I look around and notice that this particular hallway suddenly seems very empty. I could be in trouble.

"You know, I have a great sense of humor. But my boys here, they don't take kind to being insulted."

From behind Jimmy comes Spiccolli, his right hand man-beast. He's probably the strongest guy at Dale Bridge High. Of course, he's also as dumb as a rock.

"Spiccolli, what do you think of Eric here?"

Spiccolli opens his mouth, revealing a straight line of yellow teeth.

"This guy isn't so funny", he says. "He ain't no Jimmy Fallon."

The two other members of the J-Gang both laugh nervously again.

I better make my exit.

"Hey guys, I have to go."

"So soon?" Jimmy asks.

Why are these guys giving me so much attention today?

I turn to leave, but Spiccolli steps right in front of me. The big lug is blocking my only way out now. His appearance is more frightening because of his eyes which give off a calm presence, dead calm that is. You don't really know if he's going to shake your hand or knock off you head. Although I have a pretty good idea of what he's planning to do in this situation.

I reach in my pocket to see if I have anything to defend myself with. A spoon. Perfect.

"So what do we do about this?" Jimmy asks.

He takes a step towards me.

In a quick instant, I grab the trusty spoon out of my pocket and smack Jimmy across the face with it.

He screams as I than do a 360 spin and then bring the spoon across his face again.

Another member of the J-Gang, Sean, comes at me next. I duck a wild swing and catch him off guard with a high kick that sends him crying to the floor.

"That's compliments of Jaden Smith from Karate Kid!"

Louis comes at me next, tackling me to the ground and swinging a right hook with amazing force. Luckily, he misses my head by an inch and shatters his knuckle on the ground.

He howls in pain as I backslap him with the spoon. He falls to the ground, unconscious.

I turn and see that Spiccoll is still my blocking me from leaving.

"Well, there is a time for diplomacy, and a time for action. And diplomacy is dead!"

I kick him square in the groin, and then slap him with the spoon. He suddenly shows more emotion than ever before as he falls to the ground with a look of disbelief.

I look at Jimmy who is slowly getting back to his feet.

"I don't start things, I finish them! Don't mess with me again, you hear?"

I turn and walk away, leaving them struggling to discover what just happened to them.

"So what are we going to do here?"

Oh no. My mind snaps back to reality, leaving the daydream

behind. I find myself still being surrounded by the J-Gang.

My right hand moves towards my back pocket where the spoon is located. I don't pull it out though. This isn't the Matrix. The spoon is a solid eating utensil, but what was it really going to do against four people? Maybe if I was Jackie Chan I could pull it off.

So my fate is in Jimmy's hands. He looks at Spiccolli and then back at me.

"Let him go, Spiccolli. We have to get to the pep rally."

Spiccolli groans as he steps out of my way.

"It's your lucky day McKay."

"Yeah, well, guess I'll see you guys later."

I don't waste any time walking away. It's only when I'm far down the hall that I stop to wonder why they had let me go. I could have reported them to the administration, but I'm lacking credibility since I'm now a convicted school skipper. I'm surprised they didn't leave me for dead.

Mr. Edwards is standing by his office when I walk by.

"Remember, no more missed classes", he warns me. "You better hurry or you'll be late for the pep rally."

"Right", I say as I continue walking.

I'm tempted to skip the pep rally and leave school, but I

remember I've told Kenny that I would meet him there.

9

I walk into the gymnasium and see the entire school sitting in the bleachers. It's quite a sight. The freshmen sit in the bottom rows, followed by the sophomores, juniors, and finally on the top two rows the seniors. I make my way up the crowded bleachers, trying not to step on anyone's hands as I pass. As I walk by, I notice that nearly every student at Dale Bridge High seems to have a smart phone. I make sure to keep my 1998 flip phone in my pocket.

I see Tracy sitting with some friends on the far right of the top bleacher. To the far left I spot Kenny sitting next to some gothic girl. I take a seat next to him.

"I'm surprised you actually showed up." He says.

"Are you kidding? I love pep-rallies."

"You do?"

"Well, no."

"So your text said the blind date was a disaster?"

"More than you know."

"Ouch. Well, it's good to see you in school again."

"You're going to be seeing me here a lot more. Mr. Edwards told me I'm on academic probation."

"I knew something like that was going to happen. You were missing too much class."

"I'll deal with it."

I look down a few rows and see Jamie sitting with Jimmy. I nudge Kenny.

"I can't believe it's lasted this long."

"High school? It has been a long four years."

"No, I'm talking about Jamie and Jimmy."

"Oh."

The band sits in the corner of the gym playing what sounds like that Kelly Clarkson song, "Don't You want to Stay."

I'm about to make fun of this fact to Kenny when I suddenly hear him singing.

"Don't you want to hold each other tight? Don't you want to fall asleep with me tonight!"

"Ok", I say simply as I look back down to the gym. Mr. Edwards walks up to the podium and taps on the microphone.

"Testing, can everybody hear me?"

The students boo. He adjusts the microphone.

"Is this better?"

A few cheers, lots of boo's.

"May I have everybody's attention? I want to first welcome everybody to what I feel is going to be a memorable school year for all of us at Dale Bridge High."

The students are mostly quiet now.

"I wanted to take a moment to update all of you on the status of your fellow classmate Samantha. The authorities have told me that while they haven't found her, they are following up on a few leads and are hopeful of the outcome."

"Typical", I say to Kenny.

"Now let's get to some positive news. We are a school that prides itself on our sports teams. And I want to introduce these wonderful athletes to you right now. First up, I want to acknowledge the contributions of Dale Bridge's wonderful Chess Team!"

Exactly two people in the audience clap. The six members of the chess team stand proudly for six seconds until somebody pushes them away.

"And now let's hear it for the football team that nobody in our district can contain, the Dale Bridge Bulldogs!"

There is a HUGE applause from the audience. The students go crazy as members from the football team run out of the locker room. They seem to be extremely hyper. At this point, Jimmy leaves Jamie's side and joins his football team friends.

"Now this is what I call school spirit", Kenny says.

"This is what I call steroid abuse", I answer.

"Do you want to go to the party at Craig Colgate's house tomorrow night?"

"I'll pass, but have fun."

I see Jimmy walk to the front of everybody as Mr. Edwards invites him to the podium.

"Jimmy, why don't you tell the school what you're going to do to Forest Green at the homecoming game?"

Jimmy steps to the podium and looks out at the students with what I would describe as menace in his eyes.

"Forest Green is in big trouble!"

The students go nuts.

"We're going to pulverize them!"

Big cheers.

"We're going to humiliate them!"

Even louder cheers.

"We're going to slice off their heads and kick them through the uprights!"

Monstrous cheers!

"What the hell?" I say to Kenny under all the cheers. "What is wrong with our school?"

"What do you mean?"

"Jimmy is up there talking about committing mass homicide and these people are cheering."

"He wasn't being literal. He was being figurative, just generic trash talk."

"Slicing off their heads seems pretty specific."

For some unknown reason, the band starts playing the Breakfast club theme song.

Mr. Edward is back on the microphone.

"Please everybody, exit in a courteous manner, and one row at a time!"

"I'm out of here", I say.

The second floor is quiet as I make my way towards room 202.

This is where my first meeting with the math club is supposed to take place.

The door is already open, so I walk in. The room looks like all the others at Dale Bridge High. A big square shaped facility with cheap wooden desks that seems to be made from the same producers of the balsa wood bed at my house. I take a quick look around. It is completely empty, except for a strange man in a dark blown cloak standing near the chalk board.

Wait a minute.

"I'm sorry; I must have the wrong room"

I walk back outside of the room and look at the number.

202.

Well, this is the right room.

I walk back in.

"Excuse me; I'm looking for the math club."

Whoever it is seems to be a pretty big Stars Wars fan. He has a big, long cloak, covering his entire body and a hood covering his face

He's not answering me. I'm half expecting this person to crank out a light saber and pluck off my head. They instead point to a desk, I suppose wanting me to sit down.

"I should probably tell you, I'm essentially a complete novice in

Algebra. I mean I've paid attention to a few lectures, but it's always seemed like a lost cause. It normally just goes in and out."

No response. I keep speaking.

"But I'm on academic probation now. I have to conquer Algebra or I may not graduate."

Complete silence.

"Any help you can give me would be appreciated."

The cloaked figure remains motionless.

There are just too many weird things happening to me this week.

The dark figure suddenly reaches for his hood and pulls it back, revealing himself.

The first thing I notice is that he's old. Beyond a wrinkled face, he has long hair that is half jet black and half gray.

"Erick Mckay." He says in a deep voice.

Maybe people are hiding in the closet, waiting to jump out and laugh at me as soon as I buy into any of this. But where have they gotten this old guy from?

I'm forgetting to respond to him I realize.

"That's me. Who are you?"

He definitely isn't a student. He is big enough to be an NBA player if he possesses any coordination.

"My name is Reece Hicks", the man says slowly with a stone cold look.

I gulp slowly.

"Are you the janitor?"

The man looks down at me and for the first time shows an angry facial expression.

I estimate that he is at least forty years old. His voice carries quite the oomph.

"I am here to tell you about your destiny." He says.

"Listen, do you think we could talk about this tomorrow? I kind of wanted to show that I was serious about Algebra and then be on my way."

"I'm afraid that's not possible."

"I appreciate your sense of urgency, really I do, but I really think I need to get home. My mom gets worried if I'm out past three. She may call the police and have a search squad out for me."

He doesn't respond.

"Well, I'll be going than."

I stand up and walk towards the door.

Suddenly I feel an impact on the back of my legs.

And pain.

I'm in the air.

"What??" I hear myself yelp.

I land on the ground elbows first.

I sit up halfway and try to gather my bearings.

"What was that?"

I look up and see the man with the mixed hair standing in a fighting position with what appears to be a samurai sword in his hand.

He strikes a pose and then swiftly and quickly places the sword back in his cloak.

I rub my elbow and get back to my feet.

"I didn't wish to resort to violence, but I couldn't allow you to leave."

"And a tap on the shoulder didn't seem like the way to go?"

He doesn't seem very sorry as the pain in my elbow starts to melt away.

"My methods are inconsequential. The sword served its purpose as you are still here."

"I should call the police. That was assault."

"Listen to me Eric, this is very important. We don't have much time. You have been chosen."

"For what? To fail Algebra? What did you do with the math

club?"

"This town is in grave danger."

"I already know about the Starbucks their building downtown."

"You must help us, Eric."

I give a sarcastic nod and put a hand on my stomach as I let out a fake laugh.

Reece doesn't seem to appreciate my mockery as he looks around in bewilderment.

He snaps his neck.

"She thought you could be persuaded with a cup of coffee, but now I see that you're going to need more evidence."

"She?"

'You met her yesterday."

Kelly. Of course! But she didn't offer me any coffee.

"Oh, you mean the girl with the green eyes. "

"Yes."

"Where is she anyways?"

"She is busy. Now, if you will come with me I will show you why you must help us."

"Go with you? I don't even know you."

"I am Reece Hicks."

"Yes. I know your name. But a name doesn't' really mean a whole lot these days.   There is already a girl missing. How can I trust you?"

"I am vowed to protect under the oath of Zugante!"

"Zugante? What is that"?

He cracks the briefest of smiles before turning serious again.

"I am just kidding. There is no Zugante."

"Ok, so how exacty can you show me what you're talking about?"

"I'll take you to them."

"Them?'

"They are already here."

"I'm sure they are."

He walks towards the door and stands in the doorway looking at me.

"Does this have anything to do with the ghost at my house?"

He doesn't answer. This must be related. Maybe he can help?

"I hope I don't regret this",   I say walking towards the door.

A moment later we are walking in the parking lot.

"I have an automobile", he says. "We also can walk. It isn't very far."

"How far is it?"

"Three and a half miles."

"Which car is yours?"

We come to a Blue Chevy Nova. The same one that was following me and that was parked at my house.

"This is your car?"

He climbs into the driver's seat.

"You've been following me!"

"Get in." He yells with the window down.

I cautiously take a seat on the passenger side and we make our way out of the parking lot.

I turn on the radio but no stations will play.

"This car was a good choice. You'll save a lot on gas mileage."

"Secure your seatbelt!"

"Alright, you don't have to yell. So you've been following me?"

"Yes. The last few days we've been watching you. There has been good reason for it."

I'm just hoping that Reece can help me get rid of the evil spirit at my house.

Or maybe he is the ghost.

We drive three and half miles, making two right turns before coming to what appears to be an abandoned warehouse.

"Are you sure this is the place?"

He unbuckles his seatbelt and steps outside of the car. He then pulls what looks like an IPhone out of his cloak.

"My radar indicates that this is the location".

I get out of the car and look at the device in his hands.

"Did Apple make your radar?"

He looks emotionless as he begins walking towards the warehouse. I follow him.

We are very close to the front door when he suddenly holds his hand out in front of me.

"We must not approach from the front, too much danger. Let us go to the back."

"Danger? What kind of danger?"

"Trouble."

"Do you mean like Saved by the Bell, resolved by the end of the episode type trouble?"

"No."

We walk around to the back of the huge warehouse that is in the middle of nowhere.

He holds a finger to his mouth, indicating that he wants me to be quiet.

We come to a window as Reece stands in front of me, staring inside.

He then ducks down and pulls me to the ground before I can see what's inside.

"What is it? The circus?"

He turns to me. "This is very serious."

"Listen, I normally would be much more skeptical, but there have been some weird things happening to me the last few days."

"I want to hear about these instances. But first, I'd like you to look through the window."

"Alright, but first tell me one thing, what is with the outfit?"

"The cloak is perfect for concealing the sword."

"Oh, that makes sense. Plus anybody who thinks its weird could just chalk it up to you being a part of some occult."

"Yes, now take a look."

"Alright."

I slowly stand up but Reece stops me again.

"Whatever you see, you must not scream."

"You don't have to worry about that. I am not someone who screams easily."

I stand up slowly and peer inside.

My vision is horrible, I seriously need contacts. The inside of the warehouse starts as a blur but slowly begins to form into a crystal clear view.

What the…

A knot forms in my throat.

"Oh no!"

I scream, loud and erratically, until Reece covers up my mouth with his hand.

"What did we agree too? No screams right?"

"Yeah but I wasn't prepared for that!"

"What did you see?"

"It couldn't be what I thought I saw."

"What was it?"

"Monsters! Well, I mean, they look like humans but they're different."

He lets go of me and nods.

"Take another look."

I stand up slowly again and look inside the warehouse.

There are four things, shaped like human beings, but with hideously deformed faces. Their eyeballs reach out far in front of their heads. Their faces look badly burnt and their heads are covered with green, oozy hair. Maybe they were humans once, but now they are some type of genetic mutations.

I turn from the window.

"Are they Zombies?"

"That is one word for them. They are the undead. You could call them monsters, or zombies"

"Zombsters! But how??" I accidentally say it louder than I should have.

"Not so loud, you'll give away our position!"

I look back inside the window.

And see that one of the zombsters is looking directly at me.

I gulp.

"Too late."

The zombsters start dancing around in excitement.

Then they are scurrying towards the window where Reece and I are.

Or where I am.

"Reece? Where are you?"

He's gone.

I'm alone.

And monsters are coming towards me.

"Forget this!"

I jump away from the window and run back to where Reece had parked. I jump across the hood, well halfway across the hood. I come to a complete stop right on the middle of it actually.

"Damn. That always works in cop movies."

I roll the rest of the way off the hood and creep into the driver's side.

"Where are the keys?" I cry as I look in the dashboard and in the visor.

Reece has them.

Where is that old man?

CRASH!

I look up and see one of the zombsters has jumped onto the windshield.

"Holy hell", I say as I duck under the steering wheel.

"YOU'RE GOING TO DIE"! The zombster screams in fairly credible English.

I clutch the front door handle and squeeze it open as I leap onto the grass.

I look up just in time to see the monster standing directly above me.

"Head or Legs" He asks

"What?"

"Chop Heads or Legs!"

"What are you??" I ask in an attempt to buy time by making small talk with the zombster.

"Gigamesh!"

"Your name is Gigamesh?"

He lunges forward, but I crawl a few steps out of the way and he jumps past me. When I'm on my feet, he is already on the other side of me.

These things are quick!

I decide I'm going to have to fight them.

When I was in Kindergarten, I chased down a bully who had been bothering me for weeks. I tackled him to the ground. I thought I was winning but he smacked me in the face and proceeded to beat my living brains in.

This is going to be vicarious revenge. And I'm serving it cold!

I pull my arm back and then swing forward with all my might.

I miss horribly, almost throwing my arm out of its socket.

The zombster can only grin before he hits me with a forearm to the face.

I sail head first to the ground.

Another one comes onto the scene. I guess they are going to split me in half like a peanut butter and jelly sandwich.

Both the zombsters are laughing now.

"You humans stupid, always running wrong direction."

I slowly get to my feet.

The zombster frowns.

And then slaps me back to the ground.

"Annoying pest, rodent, cricket!" It yells in succession. "I eat your brains!"

"I have a better idea", I say trying to reason with him. "How about we go order a pizza and watch a football game? RG3 is having a great season."

Another backhand.

The zombsters are salivating now; spit flying from their mouths as they prepare for a large order of Erick Mckay.

Then I hear the sound of a blade swooshing through the air.

I see Gigamesh cry out in pain.

The zombster to the left of me lets out a squeal as his right arm flies off.

Then I scream when one of the monsters falls to the ground right next to me.

I get to my feet quickly.

It's Reece.

He is fighting the other monster with his sword. He suddenly spins and in one motion puts his sword through the monster. The monster splits into two, both pieces falling to the grass.

They are dead.

Reece walks towards me.

"What happened to the other two?" I question.

"They ran away when they saw me."

"I'd run too. You have a giant Samurai sword."

Reece calmly puts his sword back in his cloak.

"Now do you believe?"

I lean against the car and catch my breath.

"I need some coffee."

11

We walk into Waffles Galore a few minutes later.

After making our order, Reece pulls ten dollars out of his cloak and pays for it.

We walk to a table and sit down.

"I'm sure you have questions", he says.

"Let's start with where you're from?"

He snaps his neck again.

"I am from Dale Bridge."

"Ok, let's skip the small talk. What the hell is going on?"

"Those things in the warehouse are foot monsters."

"And they come from where? "

"The Dale Bridge Cemetery."

"Oh, right out of the graves I suppose?"

"Yes. We discovered a few empty graves there a week ago. They have come to make preparations. Something evil is here, and those things are here to do its handy work."

"So they are basically errand boys?"

"Yes."

"And what is this evil thing?"

Reece looks down for a moment, suddenly seeming uncomfortable.

"Magra."

"Wait, I thought that was just a story?"

"It may be a story to your generation, but it is a very real and evil thing for mine."

"You've had some experience with Magra?"

"Yes. It was the night of the homecoming dance, thirty years ago. I didn't want to go, but I had never been to one before and I thought why not?"

"Hey that's funny, I've never been to homecoming either. That's like a parable."

"Yes, I suppose so."

Over the next few minutes, Reece tells me what happened that night long ago.

I am left speechless.

"You see now why I say it is not a story."

"So they just went crazy?"

"No, they were possessed. I saw it in their eyes afterwards. They had no idea what they had done."

"The court system disagreed with you."

"After it all happened, I stayed in town and continued searching for the truth. It seemed hopeless. I felt like I had to get away, to start fresh somewhere. I ended up eventually going to the Military. I was gone for seventeen years. But as much as I tried, I could never stop thinking about that night. And then a year ago I was given the first message."

"What message?"

"I received a letter in the mail with no return address. The letter said that Dale Bridge was a haunted town and that Magra was very much real."

"Who wrote it?"

"They claimed to be a victim of Magra. It spoke of a need for someone to protect Dale Bridge."

"So you automatically believed the letter?"

"I believe what I had always believed. That something very evil happened that night. The letter just confirmed what I already knew."

"You sure it wasn't some type of joke?"

"Nobody would do that. Besides, because of what the letter said,

I couldn't take the chance of disregarding it."

"What did it say?"

"That Magra was going to strike again at this year's homecoming dance. It said that there would be even more victims this time around than there were twenty five years ago. And it said that I was going to need help."

"Like Kelly?"

The waitress brings over two coffees.

"Yes, I recruited Kelly last year. I needed somebody on the inside at Dale Bridge High. Someone who could keep tabs of things, keep me updated on the homecoming dance. She is my second in command. There are others who will help us also."

"And the sword?"

"I bought that on a whim a few years back. I have spent many years training with it, a hobby you could call it."

"So you've been getting inside information from a ghostly pen pal."

"It doesn't matter what the source is. We have to do whatever it takes to stop anything like that from ever happening again."

"This is a lot to digest."

"Kelly told me you were a cynical person."

"Well normally I am. The thing is there have been a bunch of weird things happening to me over the last few days."

"Like what?"

"For starters I think I heard a voice in my living room telling me to 'save them'."

Reece takes a sip off the coffee and scratches his chin.

"The voice could have been talking about Homecoming."

"It makes sense now. But I just don't understand why I would be involved. I have nothing to do with any of this."

"That is not exactly true."

"What do you mean?"

"You're house."

"What about it?"

"It's the same house Sandra lived in."

I freeze.

"You would have thought the real estate people would have told my parents."

"I started watching your house after I had read that spirits liked to inhibit the places that were familiar to them when they were alive."

"You think Sandra may have been the voice I heard?"

"Yes. And we can use your house as a way to try to

communicate with her."

"Like the movie Poltergeist?"

"If we make contact with her, she may be able to help us stop Magra."

"But what if she gets angry with us?"

"What do you mean?"

"Did you ever see Paranormal Activity?"

"No."

"Ok, well in the movie some type of evil thing is in the house. And the guy starts trying to catch the evil thing on camera. And the more he films, the angrier the evil thing gets. It's like when the guy started investigating, it ticked the evil spirit off. And then at the end the evil thing kills the guy and throws him at the camera. I just don't want to end up being thrown at the camera, that's all."

"If it is Sandra's soul, I can guarantee she will help us."

"So if we don't stop Magra, what is going to happen at Homecoming? Is it going to be like the movie Carrie?"

"From what I saw the main thing that Magra likes to do is take possession of people's bodies and make them do horrible things. I also believe Magra has something to do with the girl who is missing."

"Samantha?"

"Kelly tells me she was running for homecoming queen?"

"Yeah."

"Sandra was running for homecoming queen also."

"Magra doesn't seem to like homecoming queens. Can we find her?"

"We can try. So now that you know what's going on, will you help us?"

"You just need to access to my house to try to contact Sandra?"

"We need a little bit more than that."

"What do you mean?"

"There is a way to stop Magra. I received a second letter a few weeks ago. It spoke of a spell that can send Magra away for good."

"Where did this spell come from?"

"I don't know."

"So why don't we just recite the spell be and done with it?"

Reece sighs.

"It only works if we speak it in the presence of Magra."

"You mean we actually have to confront this demon and say the spell?"

"Right."

"And he's just going to sit there idly while we recite it?"

"It's the only way."

"And what about those monsters, the town isn't exactly safe with them around."

"They may be preparing to attack at the Homecoming dance."

"So where do I come in?"

"The spell is located in the Dale Bridge Library. The letter said that the spell is written on the back cover of a book about the Watergate scandal."

"A book that no high school student would ever check out, smart. Can Kelly get to it?"

"It's too dangerous. Your school isn't safe anymore. There are people that are working for Magra. People in that library even."

"Really?"

"Yes, and they know the math club is against them. Somebody tried to run Kelly over a few days ago. She can't go back there."

"I get it. They don't know about me, so I can slip in undetected and get the spell."

"Will you help us?"

"This seems like a decision I might regret."

"Do you believe in destiny?"

"Not really. I think life is what you make it."

"A long time ago I used to think that myself. But now I think we all have a purpose."

I lean back in my seat and weigh my options.

"Why can't my mission be peaceful? Like a camping trip to Canada."

"This is the situation. You must accept it."

"But why me?"

"The letter mentioned you by name. That is how I knew to find you."

I take in a deep breathe.

"I guess I really am meant to be involved."

"I'm going to be straight with you. This is a do or die mission. You will be risking your life."

I think for a few moments. This is a big decision.

"I'm not a big fan of school or the people there. But I don't want to see everyone die."

Reece nods.

"So you're in?"

"I guess so."

"We'll meet with the team tomorrow morning."

"The team? You mean the math club?"

"Yes."

"A math club that secretly fights demons. That's just grande."

12

"So where are we going exactly?"

It is early the next day. And I do mean early. 6.30 am to be exact. I haven't been up this early since, well, never.

"We have to choose where we meet carefully."

"Absolutely."

We pull into a driveway in a typical Dale Bridge neighborhood. The garage on cue begins to open up and a familiar face comes jogging out. He seems very happy to see us.

I step out of the car and scratch my head.

"Dan Fundell."

"Where you been at dawg? Mom made brownies!"

He holds up a plate of fudge brownies, which I decline.

"Welcome to my humbled crib!"

We follow him up the driveway and into the garage.

I see Kenny sitting on a box using his smart phone. I

immediately walk up to him.

"Why didn't you give me a heads up about any of this?"

He looks up from his phone.

"We had a plan to stick too."

"So this is all for real right? I mean this isn't like an elaborate joke or anything?"

"You saw those things at the warehouse right?"

"I'm calling them Zombsters actually."

Dan taps me on the shoulder.

"Son, I just got the Last Air bender on DVD!"

"Well, prepare to be disappointed."

He frowns.

"Damn. I knew M. Night shouldn't have joined the Illuminati!"

The inside of the garage contains all the normal things you would expect. There is a box full of tools, a spare tire, and a few buckets of paint.

"So where is Kelly at?" I ask Reece.

Dan jumps in between us.

"Do you any of you guys want a glass of milk? And don't be afraid to ask for chocolate!"

"No thanks."

"She is late again?" Reece asks.

Reece doesn't want to begin until she arrives, and so we hang out for a few minutes. I mostly talk to Dan Fundell about the downfall of M. Night Shylahams career.

"Hey", I say, "I liked Sixth Sense as much as anybody, but the guy peaked with his first two movies."

"You didn't like the Village!? Are you serious?"

"The ending of the Village was right out of Sesame Street. And don't get me started on Lady in the Water."

"Those were both the bomb!"

Dan takes a bite out of a brownie.

"Seriously dude, the Village and Transporter 2 are my favorite movies of all time."

I sigh.

"Transporter 2? I would like to transport that movie back to being an idea that never materializes."

"Son, I totally can't believe your taste in movies man!"

"We'll agree to disagree."

I hear the noise of an engine as I look towards the front of the garage and see a car pulling into the driveway.

"Is that her?" I ask Dan.

"Yeah son, that's her car."

I make it out to be an Acura RSX. The engine sounds like it's had some work done on it.

We see her get out of the car, a shadow first, and then a body. She casually walks into the garage.

I meet her halfway. She doesn't look too excited to see me.

"Gone with the Wind", I say.

"What does that mean?"

"You were reading it earlier."

"So?"

"Scarlett, the main character in it, has green eyes also."

"I know that."

"So your eyes are officially in the category of full blown interesting now."

"Doesn't that just make my day?"

"That's a great car", I say.

"It was a present from my mom."

"She sounds nice."

"She isn't." She answers coldly.

"How can you be late again?" Reece asks.

"I got held up at home, sorry."

I notice she still has the light jacket on.

"I've filled Eric in on almost everything", Reece says.

"Good", she answers simply. "Let's get to the details."

Reece coughs and then starts speaking.

"So the plan is that Eric is going to get the book we need from the library."

"Do they know about Eric?" Kenny asks.

"I'm not positive but I don't think so." Reece answers. "Either way we'll have to take that chance."

"That's encouraging", I say

"They likely have someone guarding the book, maybe indirectly. You have to be very careful."

"So what if I do get confronted by someone?"

"Then you pretend that your a student who just happens to be highly interested in Watergate. We're going to have Kenny hanging right outside the library. He'll keep walking by the glass door and looking in. If he sees anything suspicious he'll tell us."

"And you guys will do what, storm the library and save me?"

"We don't want to do anything until we get that book."

I nod.

"Ok, sounds simple enough. I'll try not to screw it up."

There is suddenly a lot of movement in the garage as Kelly and Reece begin walking all around the garage. Reece puts a few different devices in his pocket before handing one to me.

"This is a communication device. You can contact me at any time by holding down this button and speaking into it."

"So it's a walkie-talkie."

"What?"

"Never-mind."

I stand next to Kelly.

"You're not a big socializer are you?"

"No. Are you ready to go?"

"I don't know. This all feels like a dream."

"What are you talking about?"

"A few days ago I had no reason to be even remotely excited about life. Everything seemed purposeless. Then this whole adventure just fell into my lap. It's hard to believe that I could be a factor in any of this."

She finishes putting something in her pocket and looks at me.

"It doesn't really matter where you started. What matters is where you finish."

"That's very Zen of you. So you like all of this?"

Her expression turns somewhat grim.

"No", she says softly. "I have to go help Reece."

"Thanks. Where are you going to be during all of this?"

"I'll be around", she says before walking away.

I hear Reece call my name.

"What's up?" I call back.

"It's time. Let's go."

The tension is thick as we drive towards Dale Bridge High. I sit in the backseat with Reece and Kelly in the two front seats. Kenny is in a separate car. As I'm understanding, Dan's purpose in the group is more about using his house for meetings than anything else. I decide to try to alleviate the tension with a little bit of humor.

"Hey guys, what does every movie ever made have in common?"

They give no guesses, so I'm forced to give the answer.

"Samuel L. Jackson!"

Silence.

"You know what would be the best way to die? A hit and run by a car full of circus clowns. Can you imagine? They hit you, and they all get out of the car and look over the body very seriously. Than one of them makes a balloon animal and they all bust out laughing."

"Is the bad stand-up comedy routine really necessary?" Kelly asks.

"I thought it was alright", I say quietly.

Reece seems to be lost in deep thought, perhaps going through the different possibilities concerning what's about to happen.

The car starts to slow down as we slowly pull into the parking lot. We make our way towards a side entrance near the back of the school before the car comes to a complete stop. I wait for somebody to speak, but silence ensues.

"Well, hopefully when you guys see me again I'll have that book."

"Remember", Reece says, "the book is called Watergate Revealed. And don't forget to use the communication device if need be."

"Let's hope there is no need."

I step out of the car and head into the school.

I keep my head down as I walk past the unsuspecting kids who are concerning themselves with normal teenage matters. I was one of them just a few days ago. Now my former complaints seem completely trivial.

It isn't long before I'm outside of the library.

I look for Kenny, who is supposed to be watching my back. He's nowhere to be found which I find a bit ominous.

Well, here goes nothing, I think to myself as I open the library door and take a step inside.

We have a big library, I realize. A quick survey of the room shows that it's about half full. I guess more people read books than I had thought. I look up at the clock. 7.05 am. The official school day doesn't start for another twenty five minutes. Hopefully the forces of evil aren't early risers.

I sit down at a computer and use the search engine to find exactly where the book is located.

Non-Fiction, Section E. Well, that shouldn't be too hard to find.

I get up from the computer and walk across the library.

The sections appear to be in alphabetical order.

There it is. Section E. I turn in and slowly walk through it.

It seems normal enough, no heavy dark shadow centered on it or anything.

I begin to look closer at the books on the shelves.

Where are you, Watergate, I think to myself as I scan through the books.

"Can I help you with something?" I hear from behind me.

I turn around and see Miss Castigas, the school librarian standing behind me.

Where did she come from?

"Oh, well I think I'm ok", I answer nervously.

"Are you looking for a specific book?"

"I am, but I think I can find it myself."

She smiles.

"Well I'll be happy to wait while you find it. Than we can go to the desk and I'll help you check the book out."

"Great", I say. She isn't going to leave me alone.

Should I abort the mission?

No, I can't. If I leave now and come back later than they will know something is up. Plus, how do I know that Miss Castigas is involved? So far her actions are nothing more than that of a helpful librarian.

I look closely at the books. My fingers and eyes go through an entire row. The Watergate book should be in this row.

But it isn't.

"That's strange", I say out loud.

"What is it?"

"I'm looking for a book about Watergate. It's for a school report.

From what the computer said, it should be here."

I watch Miss Castigas's face while I say this in order to detect if there is any change in her expression at my mention of Watergate. Her smile stays consistent.

"Oh, we do have one book about Watergate, but it's checked out."

"Are you sure?"

"Yes, I believe someone actually got it yesterday. Maybe they were working on the same report as you."

"Right", I say as I back away from the shelf.

Something is definitely up. Why would the computer say it's available if it isn't?

"Well, I guess I'll just wait for whoever to return it than."

I slowly walk past her and out of section E. She watches me walk away.

I walk past her desk and stop when I see her office.

If I was protecting something, I would keep it in my office.

I turn and look back towards section E. No sign of her.

I check out the other side of the library and see her helping a student in the far right corner.

I turn and look back at the office.

I'll be in and out. Just a quick check.

I make sure no other students are looking before I slip behind the desk and grab the doorknob to the office door. I'm relieved to find the door is open. I walk in and fumble for the light switch before turning it on. It's a small but spacious office. I see her computer.

Maybe I can change my Algebra grade?

I take a seat at the desk.

Many of the school computers are old enough to have seen Ronald Reagan's inauguration speech. I see the graphic of Windows 7 come up on the screen. It would figure the faculty gets Windows while the students get a cheap imitation.

A screen opens up and reveals a desktop with all the usual Windows icons on it. Now we're in business, I think to myself. Then again, that was the easy part. What do I do now? I click on the My Computer icon, and do a quick search for the word 'grades'. It comes up with no matches.

It's right than that I hear footsteps near the door. Damn, who is that? I hop from the computer and leap towards the light switch, shutting it off. I then slide down to my knees and hide behind the door. A shadow walks by the door. Close call.

What am I feeling on my finger?

I look down and see a giant spider crawling up my hand!

"OHHHHH!" I start to gag but I put a hand over my mouth.

With no other options, I smack my hand against the wall a few times until the spider falls off.

"Get away from me spider! Go trap a worm in a web or something."

I turn the light on and start looking around the room for the book. This is taking too long, I have to hurry up and get out of here.

I hear a noise at the door again and look up. Someone is at the door again! A shadow stands there and I see the doorknob start to turn.

I quickly reach into my pocket and grab the walkie talkie.

"Houston, we have a problem", I say.

I hear a screeching noise come back from the walkie talkie.

Damn, no reception!

I look up and see the door begin to open.

I'm done for.

I stand frozen as the door opens fully and the shadowy figure becomes clear.

"Kenny!"

He walks into the room and closes the door behind him.

"Man, what is taking so you long in here?"

"I can't find the book!"

"It doesn't matter; if Miss Castigas finds us in here we're in big trouble."

"Alright, help me look for it real quick."

We both look around the room carefully.

"It's hopeless, the book isn't here", I say.

"What about there?"

Kenny points at a singular cabinet near her printer that I had previously missed.

We both walk towards it. I kneel over and pull the handle.

"Eureka!"

In the cabinet lies a paperback copy of 'Watergate Revealed'.

"Grab it and let's go!"

I pick the book up and we both cautiously stand by the door. Kenny opens it slowly and looks out before nodding.

"She must have left the library."

"Let's do the same."

We step out from the office and head towards the library exit.

Once we're outside of the library I take a deep breathe.

"We did it."

"Your right, good job."

"Now what?"

"Here's what we'll do."

Kenny turns and looks around for a moment than turns back to me.

And punches me right in the stomach.

I gasp for air as I fall to my knees. The book slips out of my hands and to the ground.

Kenny picks it up.

"Thanks for your help Eric. Magra will appreciate it."

I can't manage to talk but I look up at Kenny and see an evil smile across his face.

"I have to be going", he says. "I'll see you at the prom. It's going to be a hell of a dance."

13

"Kenny must have been there backup plan."

Reece says that as I take a seat in a chair next to both Kelly and Dan. We are all gathered back in room 202.

"Son, my mind is blown", Fundell says.

I shake my head.

"I've known the guy for a year. He's the squarest person I know. I never would have thought..."

Reece scratches his chin. "He managed to keep all of this a secret from you for some time. So it doesn't shock me that he was also able to keep his affiliation with Magra from us."

"Magra was one step ahead of us."

Kelly stands from her chair suddenly.

"What do we do now?"

I cough.

"I for one say we go to the theater and see that new horror movie, GPS-187."

"We have to get that book", Reece says.

"Yeah, but how?" I ask.

"You know where Kenny lives right?"

"I do, but if we go there his parents will call the police."

"It may be the only way."

A light bulb goes off in my head.

"Wait! I think I know where Kenny is going to be tonight."

"You do?"

"Yeah. We're going to need our party hats."

I'm standing on a front porch later in the day after school.

Jamie opens her front door after only a few knocks.

"Are you busy?" I ask.

"I was just studying, what's going on?"

"I have a crazy story to tell you."

"Oh boy."

She invites me inside and I take a seat in her living room.

"Do you want something to drink?" She asks.

"No thanks."

"So you have something you want to tell me?"

"I do. I'm going to need you to be very open-minded."

"Okay."

"Let me frame it for you first. You're a fan of Twilight right?"

"Very much so."

"Well, do you think anything like that could ever happen in real life?"

She doesn't think long.

"No."

This is going to be harder than I thought.

I take a deep breath, and then proceed to tell Jamie everything that's happened in the last few days. She seems very disbelieving at first, but once I finish the entire story she looks pretty serious.

"You're ribbing me right?"

"That's exactly what I thought at first. But, after everything I've seen, I'm a believer. Look I know it sounds ludicrous, but would I have come to your house if it wasn't serious?"

"Well, the only other time I remember you coming over is when I told you that my mom had made Peanut Butter Rice Krispies treats."

"Hey that could in normal circumstances easily be construed as serious."

"So than this is no joke?"

"It's more serious than a Daniel Craig facial expression."

"And this Magra thing is going to attack the students at the dance?"

"From what I understand, Magra will make it so that the students attack the students at the dance."

She takes a moment to pace around the room before coming to a stop.

"I believe you, I guess."

"Really?"

"You've never lied to me before. And I don't think you're crazy."

I stand from her couch.

"I'm glad you believe me. Because I need your help."

"What can I do?"

"Well, I don't want you to be directly involved in any of this. It's too dangerous. I just wanted to see if you could get me into that party tonight. It's invite only and I think Kenny is going to be there. If we can't get that book from him, things could get pretty bad tommorrow night."

"I'm going to the party. You could ride with us if you want."

"Us? You mean you and Jimmy?"

"Yes."

"I don't know. Jimmy and I aren't the best of friends."

"Whatever you feel towards him can't be stronger than wanting to save the school right?"

"Well."

She stares at me incredulously.

"Fine. For the sake of the school I'll try to get along with him."

There is a knock at her door.

We both look at each other.

"Are you expecting anybody? Maybe a pizza or something?"

She shakes her head.

The knock comes again.

"Why don't you look out the window", I say.

"Why don't you do that and I'll wait over there." She points to her kitchen.

"Ok, fair enough. I guess if it is something bad it's only here because of me."

The doorbell rings a third time.

"Should I call the police?" She asks.

"No way. We can't involve the authorities in any of this. Besides, now is not the time to panic. Grab a butcher's knife from the kitchen and I'll answer the door."

A moment later, with a knife if my hand, I extend my arm towards the door. I'm shaking with goose bumps as I reach for the doorknob. I grip it and slowly turn it counter clockwise. I look at Jamie.

"Here goes", I say.

I flip the door open fast

Jamie screams.

"Hey, why are you screaming?" I ask

She stops screaming and looks at me. Then she looks outside and back to me.

"Nobody is out there", she says surprisingly.

"It's what a horror director would call a false scare."

Just than a figure appears the door. This time I scream.

"AHHHHHHHHHHH!"

Jamie grabs me and puts her hand over my mouth.

"My parents are upstairs."

I look at the figure in the doorway.

"Kelly! How did you find me?"

She steps in and looks at both of us.

"Reece put a tracker on you before you left school, remember?"

"You were checking on me? That's sweet of you."

Jamie coughs.

"Oh, sorry. Kelly, this is my friend Jamie. She's going to help us get into that party.""

Kelly shakes her head.

"You shouldn't have told her. She's in danger now."

"Under the present circumstances I didn't see any other way."

"You could have just told her that you wanted to go to the party."

"Oh, well yeah I guess I could have done it that way."

Jamie puts a hand up. "He doesn't usually go to parties; I would have inquired why he was suddenly interested."

"That's true", I say. "The last party I went to was at Chucky Cheese."

"Jimmy and I are leaving for the party around eight."

"Great. Kelly and I will tag along. Once we're inside, we'll look for Kenny."

Kelly steps back onto the porch. "I'll be ready", she says.

I cough. "On the brightside, if any of this gets publicized we may be able to get one of those ghost hunter shows on television."

I spend a lot longer than usual making sure I look alright for the party. It sounds superficial, I know. But it is after all my first and likely only high school party.

I pour a cup of mouthwash and let it sit in my mouth for a few minutes until it starts to burn. I also wash some crust out of my eyes before exiting the bathroom. As I walk into the living room, I see Kelly standing around looking bored.

I smile. "Let's party!"

She shakes her head as we hear the doorbell ring.

I open the door and see Jimmy standing there. I never would have guessed I'd be getting picked up for a party by Jimmy Winston. He looks to be just as surprised by this turn of events as I am

"Mckay, you guys ready?"

"Yeah, we are. Thanks for giving us a ride."

"It wasn't my idea Mckay."

"Right."

As we head out the door I can't help but notice that Jimmy is completely iced out. It seemed like he had watched a Lil Wayne music video, and had tried to imitate the wardrobe to the best of his ability. He has a fake diamond necklace on, as well as a diamond watch, and even though it's dark outside, he is wearing designer sunglasses.

Jamie is waiting in her car as we all jump in.

Kelly and I of course take the backseat, leaving shotgun for Jimmy.

"Hello", Jamie says cheerfully.

"Howdy", I say in response.

As we drive away, there is an uncomfortable silence that takes over the car. This is a group of people that really don't know each at all. Luckily, Jamie breaks the silence at the first red light.

"Do we have a plan?" She asks.

I wonder how much she's told Jimmy about all of this.

"Yes. My plan is to find a date for Homecoming", I say.

Jimmy turns and looks back at me. He takes off his sunglasses.

"You don't have to play dumb. Jamie told me about the whole demon thing."

Kelly shakes her head.

"Did she?" I say slowly.

"I laughed when she told me. You have a crazy imagination."

"Yeah, well, we just need you guys to get us into the party. We'll go do our own thing from there."

"I bet", Jimmy says as he turns back around.

"So where is the J-Gang tonight?"

Jimmy laughs.

"You actually call them the J-Gang?"

"Sure, don't you?"

"No. That's something the scabs around school came up with."

"Scabs, right."

I lean back in my seat and look over at Kelly.

"Have you been to a lot of parties?" I ask.

"Not really", she answers.

I nod. "Same here."

We arrive at the party a few minutes later. These parties are the calling card for Craig Colgate. It has become a tradition every year at Dale Bridge High. I can only assume that his parents are always out of town when these parties take place.

It's a little house on top of a hill with no neighboring houses in sight. As we pull up, I notice the street leading up to the house is packed with vehicles. The parking jobs are all bad enough to suggest a teen party.

The only parking spot we can find requires a little bit of a walk. We follow the paved trail all the way to the front door of the house. It is a decently sized house, not too big, but just the right size for a house party. And the location is appealing because Craig doesn't have to worry about the neighbors calling the police on him.

We are let in by a door man who looks surprised to see us.

"Hey, you folks must be slumming it tonight?"

"That's us", I say as we walk through the front door, I hear music loud enough to shake the house at its foundation. I see a few eyes staring at us as we stroll into the living room, probably because Jimmy is with us. There are a couple of kids I recognize from school dancing on the marble floor. The carpet has been rolled up and is perched against the wall. A couple of couches lay next to the marble floor, producing a sitting area that seems to be far too overcrowded at this moment.

"Let's see what kind of food they have", Jimmy says.

We walk into the kitchen, where much to my surprise, there is a guy making a Peanut Butter and Jelly sandwich. I stand in front, watching this guy dig into the refrigerator looking for a carton of milk to go with his sandwich. After the guy pours a glass of milk, he grabs the sandwich and the glass and starts to walk out of the kitchen. Upon passing, he momentarily stops and looks at me.

"Hey dude, do you want half?" He asks as he takes a monster bite and starts chewing.

"Actually, I'm fine", I answer.

We all hang in the kitchen and survey the room.

"Everyone is here", Jamie says.

I search the room. "Do you see Kenny anywhere?"

"Right there", Kelly points him out to us. He's dancing with some girl on the other side of the room, with a drink in his hand.

"So now that he's evil he's getting girls?"

"He definitely has more pep in his step", Jamie says.

"What now?" I ask.

Jimmy takes Jamie by the hand. "We're going to go dance. See you guys later."

They walk away as I turn to Kelly.

"He's right there in plain sight, we can't get to him like this."

Kelly nods.

"We just need to wait for him to get a little bit tipsy. It will be easier to get information from him if he doesn't have his inhibitions."

"Good thinking."

She starts to walk away.

"Hey, where are you going?"

"I'm going to make sure everything else is on the up and up."

"What am I supposed to do?"

"Mingle", she answers. "You said you wanted to find a date for homecoming."

She walks away. I can't help but admire her intelligence and take action attitude.

But what does she think about me?

I haven't been able to decipher her feelings because all our conversation has been about this whole demon business. Maybe I should ask her out if we survive this whole ordeal. I mean, what do I really have to lose?

Pride, self-respect, and a big hole in my ego, that's what.

But I don't have much of that stuff anyway.

A guy walks into the kitchen with a beer in his hands.

"Hey, you don't look like a regular."

"Are you kidding? I've been to more parties than Lindsey Lohan."

The guy takes a sip from the beer and belches as he walks away.

I turn and see a girl suddenly standing to me. It's like she's come out of the wall. I take a place standing next to her and notice her as a member of the girl's volleyball team. She is leaning up against the wall, and seems to be incredibly bored. It may be a good time for me to secure that homecoming date.

"Hi', I say. "I've seen you somewhere before?"

I note that she has a drink in her hand.

"Maybe at school?" She answers.

"Oh yeah, that makes sense. My name is Eric."

"I'm Erica", she answers.

"That's kind of funny." And weird, I think. An Eric dating an Erica almost seems like I would be dating my cousin.

"Some party huh?" She says.

"Yeah. I'm kind of disappointed with the lack of cake. I mean, what party doesn't have cake?"

She laughs and says "good point."

If I can only figure out what she's drinking.

"What's your favorite drink?" She asks, seemingly reading my mind.

"Fruitopia."

A strange look comes across her face.

"You mean, like Fruitopia mixed with Vodka?"

I cough. "Actually, I mean just Fruitopia by itself."

And with that comment, she walks away, without saying a word.

"Hey wait", I call, "was it something I said?"

Maybe she doesn't like Fruitopia?

It doesn't matter. I see what would be a much more impressive homecoming date, Tracy Winters, standing near the stereo. I mess around with my hair for a second, hoping that one of the strands isn't sticking out awkwardly like Alph-Alpha. And then I'm off, heading towards the height of success or the bottom of rejection. Tracy is the hottest free agent at the party. Maybe she's willing to take her talents down to Eric Ville?

I stop just a few feet in front of her.

"Hello there", I say with a high tone. Great, I sound like Mark Hamill from Star Wars.

"Hi Eric, how are you?" She asks.

She knows my name! I have to calm down.

"I'm good, how are you?"

"Just enjoying the party", she answers.

Good conversation is truly an art that takes a while to master. A great conversationalist can come through in any situation, always having something interesting to say when the conversation has seemed to dry out.

I'm not that guy, at least not with the really popular girls. But I have to make this conversation work. And it's all about what I say next.

"Hey, I was wondering if I could borrow a pen."

What the f***? That's the best I can come up with?

I deserve rejection.

"I do." She thankfully enough has a pen in his purse and hands it to me.

Where do I go from here?

Fortunately, she speaks again a moment later.

"Hey, you were in my drama class right?"

"Yes." Thank goodness for small miracles.

"Did you like it?"

"Sure."

"It was an easy A", she says.

I don't want to tell her that I actually got a C.

"Yeah", I agree. "Hey speaking of that, did you ever see that movie Easy A?"

It seemed like a good transition in my mind.

"No."

Well, that was a fail. Wait, I need to stay positive.

"So what did you do last weekend?"

What a stupid question. It's already Thursday, why would I be asking about last weekend? By my count, I'm so far coming off as both boring and desperate.

"I went to a museum."

"Wow, so you had a legit weekend."

"My dad works at a museum in DC, so we go up there once a month."

"That's cool. I ordered a pizza from Sam's Pizza"

"Those are good."

"I guess. Hey, I wanted to tell you that you were great in the school play."

A smile lights up across her face. I'm not sure if anybody has ever complimented her as an actress.

"Thanks, it was so many lines to remember."

"I can imagine. I auditioned for that play also."

"You didn't get a part?'

"Well, not the part I wanted. I wanted the lead role but they offered me the role of peasant number three."

"Oh."

"So I know you used to volunteer at the school planetarium. Are you into stars and things like that?"

I am hoping that a discussion of astronomy is not about to take place, as I lack the knowledge to really participate.

"Sort of, so what brings you to a party?" She asks. She must see through the facade and recognize that I'm not a party person.

"I'm trying to get more out of my life, I guess."

"That's good", she says as she looks ahead.

Alright, enough of the small talk. I need to complete my mission.

"Listen, I wanted to ask you something."

"Yes?"

"Are you going to Homecoming with anybody?"

The moment of truth.

She looks at me and immediately responds.

"Yes."

I force a smile. "I didn't know you were seeing anybody."

"I sort of am. I don't know, he just asked me."

Beat to the punch, damn.

"Who?"

"Kenny."

Son of a bitch. The evil has given him the swag of a thousand celebrities.

"Well, have fun." I say as I make my exit.

I walk back over near the kitchen and see Jamie standing there alone.

"What was that all about?" Jamie says.

"What do you mean?"

"You were talking to Tracy?"

"Yeah, trying to get a date for homecoming."

"And?"

"And I'm still trying. She's going with Kenny."

"Wow, what about Kelly?"

"I don't think Kenny is taking Kelly to the dance."

"No, I mean why don't you ask Kelly to the dance?"

"You think?"

"Yeah, she's cute."

"I suppose so. Do you think she would say yes?"

"You won't know until you try."

"Not once has that phrase ever actually inspired confidence in someone."

"Just do it. You know, I would like you to have what Jimmy and I have."

"Geez. You really like the guy huh?"

"Yes."

"Alright, I'll ask her at some point tonight. Where is she anyways?"

"She's dancing with Kenny!"

"What?"

I turn and see what Jamie is seeing. They are on the dance floor alright. In fact, they are discussing something.

"I'll be back", I say.

I walk towards the dance floor. This is some great undercover work that Kelly is doing. But I want to make sure there is nothing more to it than that.

Soon I'm at a point where I'm on the dance floor standing right next to them. Now everybody else on the dance floor is of course dancing, so a guy just standing there with a smoldering expression on his face is more than just noticeable. Kenny sees me first, with Kelly than catching my eye a moment later.

They stop dancing and separate. Kelly as usual has no expression on her face as she steps to the side.

"Hey how are you man?" Kenny says as if nothing has changed in our friendship.

I grin.

"My stomach hurts, likely a result of you punching me there.

"Sorry about that man. I had to get the book from you."

"Why Kenny, why are you working for the forces of evil?"

"You call it evil; I call it the powerful side."

"I thought you were a good dude."

He laughs.

"I would rather be bad and alive than good and dead."

"I'd rather be good and alive myself."

"What do you want Anthony?"

"A gold brick, a date for the homecoming, maybe just the book you stole from me?"

"I don't think I can help you with any of those things?"

"So I'm going to have to take the book from you, is that it?"

"Didn't I just beat you up a little while ago?"

"You tried, but I'm still here, smiling and everything."

"You want me to finish you off, is that it? I suggest you go about your business."

I step forward.

"I'm making this my business."

I had heard that line in many action movies, and had always wanted to use it. There was no better opportunity than this.

"Some people don't know when to go away and stay away." Kenny says.

"I just want to know, has Magra given you any backup? Or are you on your own?"

"I don't need any help to take out the likes of you."

I look at Kelly who slowly walks away.

Where is she going?

I talked tough, but in my head I know that Kenny himself could probably take me in a fight. He is a few inches taller than me and is pretty strong.

"So you want to do this?"

"Yes, but not here. All of these people, they're the main course at the dance if you get what I'm saying. But I can make sure that you don't even make it to the dance. So if you got all this new courage in you, why don't you meet me at the Dale Bridge Cemetery in an hour?"

I hesitate and cough but then I look him straight in the eyes.

"You got it."

14

I walk over to where Jamie and Jimmy are standing.

"Guys, I need a ride to the cemetery."

"And why is that Mckay?" Jimmy asks.

"Kenny challenged me to a fight and I accepted."

"Why would you fight at the cemetery?" Jamie asks. "Doesn't he have Magra on his side?"

"Yeah, but going by what he said it sounded like he was willing to face me alone."

Kelly appears suddenly out of nowhere.

"You can't trust him", she says. "He's an expert liar, remember?"

"I know, but we can't attack him here at the party in front of all these people. At least at the cemetery we have options."

"And what if this is all a trap?"

"The dance is tomorrow. We don't have time for what if."

Jimmy laughs. "I can't believe you guys are still pitching this story."

I look at Jamie. "This is serious."

She turns to Jimmy.

"Can we give them a ride?"

"I've been drinking!" He says

"I'll drive", she offers.

He groans. "Talk about a wild goose chase."

I turn to Kelly. "Let's do this."

"I don't think this is such a good idea", Jamie says.

"You know something; you're just like Chucky from Rugrats."

"What?"

"You remember how Tommy always wanted to go on adventures, and Chucky would always be in the background saying 'I don't think this is such a good idea'."

"I think you're the only one who watched Rugrats."

"Well regardless, we can corner Kenny in the cemetery and get some answers out of him."

"I'm just giving you suckers a ride", Jimmy says as he heads towards the door.

We all load into Jimmy's Honda Accord and take off towards the cemetery. I'm in the back seat with Kelly while Jimmy and Jamie stare ahead in the front seat.

Jamie turns her head and looks at us in the back seat.

"You're really going to fight him?"

"I can try negotiating with him first, but my hunch is that won't do us any good."

Jamie looks over at Kelly.

"So Kelly, I've never seen you around school."

Kelly seems to be mentally disengaged as she turns towards Jamie.

"I don't think we hang in the same social circle."

"Mine is like a social triangle", I say. "Or at least it was."

Jimmy chuckles. "I can't believe I'm hanging with you guys."

He looks over at Jamie. "The things I do for love", he says.

We soon park at the cemetery and strategize.

"We're going to have to jump him", I say.

"You can't be serious", Jamie says.

"The fate of the school is at stake. Extreme situations call for extreme measures."

"What if he's destroyed the book?" Jamie asks.

"There isn't any way for us to know. I'll distract him, and then all you guys get him from behind. We can tie him up."

"Do you have any rope?"

"No."

"Then that plan is a fail."

"Hey at least I came up with a plan."

Kelly sighs. "We're wasting time."

She steps out of the car first, and we all follow suit, except for Jimmy that is.

Jamie tells us to hold on for a second and spends about a minute arguing with Jimmy. Finally, he steps out of the car and joins us.

"We appreciate the help", I say to Jimmy.

"Let's get this over with", he replies. "I got things to do."

We begin walking. Luckily, the cemetery gate is unlocked. We walk right in and I see a full moon staring down at us from the sky.

"So what's the plan?" Jamie asks.

"We find Kenny and ask him what he knows. If he doesn't want to tell us, we get forceful with him. That's where you come in Jimmy."

Jimmy stops. "What are you talking about?"

"You know how to be intimidating. We need you to be the muscle here."

He looks at Jamie. "This is unbelievable", he says.

"You know, the four of us should come up with a name for our group", I suggest.

"We're not a group", Jimmy says. "This is a one and done deal."

I nod. "I'm not saying we have to have countless sequels. But for this one occasion we are a couple of high school crime fighters. The Dale Bridge High Gazette will have to publish a story about us after we save the school."

"They'll never know anything about this", Kelly says.

"So we're going to do all of this and get no credit or recognition?"

"That's right."

"Damn."

Jamie shakes her head. "The school is in danger, how could you be thinking about your reputation?"

"It would be a nice side benefit at least. Hey, how about we call ourselves the Math Club?"

"I'm not in no stinking Math Club", Jimmy complains.

"Yeah", Jamie says, "we haven't done enough to warrant a name anyways. We're closer to the Babysitter's Club than crime fighters."

"Or that show Ghost Writer", I say.

The pathway in the cemetery is about as creepy as you would expect.

"Man, can you believe this fog out here tonight? It's just like that movie."

"Which one?" Jimmy asks.

"The Fog."

"Oh."

"He's got to be here somewhere", Kelly says.

We walk slowly, carefully, each footstep making a light noise.

"This is usually the part of a scary movie where someone jumps out."

"Do you have to say that?" Jamie asks.

"I'm just bracing you guys, I mean I know horror movies, and this is almost always when something big happens."

"Those are movies, not real life."

"Hey, you don't know, this could be a movie, or even a book.

Someone could be sitting behind a computer deciding your fate at this very moment Jamie."

"You have issues", she replies.

And then we see him.

"What the hell is this?"

It's Kenny. He's standing by a grave and he doesn't look very happy.

"Well", I begin. "Let me be the first to introduce you to the Math Club!"

Everybody else stays quiet.

"You couldn't face me alone, is that it? Do you see any of my friends here?"

"I thought I was your friend. You have new friends now? Are they evil?"

"We weren't friends you sucker, I just used you."

"Well you still have my Madden. And I better get it back in good condition!"

Kelly then suddenly steps in front of me.

"Kenny, Magra has possessed you. But you need to realize that he's only using you."

"Who in the hell are you and why are you talking to me?"

"That's not important."

I nudge Jamie. "She really doesn't like giving out her name unless she has too."

"All the rest of you losers need to go home", Kenny says. "I came here for a one on one with Eric."

I speak up again. "I brought them because I couldn't trust that you would be alone. This felt like a trap. I don't know how much you know about Magra's plans, but are you aware that people are going to die at Homecoming tomorrow unless you give us that book?"

He laughs. "I'm counting on it."

"Wow, you really are evil", I say.

"Do you want to see how evil I am?"

"Are you going to show me your late fees from the library?"

"No, I have something better for you."

Suddenly, Kenny's eyes begin to turn Bright red.

"Good job Eric", I hear Jamie say.

"What's happening to him?" Jimmy asks.

Kenny's whole body starts shaking and soon his hair sticks straight up.

"He's turning into something", I say. "And whatever it is spells trouble for us."

We all step back as Kenny's face turns into a red, bloody crimson mask.

"Here's Kenny"! He yells as blood begins to drip from his face.

I look at everyone else.

"So I don't think our plan is working out."

"Can we leave', Jamie asks frantically.

Kenny laughs as blood flies from his face. "Oh by the way Eric, you remember how you thought that this felt like a trap?"

"Yeah?"

"You have great intuition. I'm expecting company."

"You are?"

"And my company isn't exactly bringing flowers and candy."

He points towards the entrance of the cemetery.

And that's when we all see them.

About four Zombsters headed our way.

"They're very hungry", Kenny laughs.

"What the hell are those?" Jimmy asks.

I scratch my chin nervously.

"Jimmy, you know how Tupac is your favorite rapper?"

"Yeah?"

"Well, I think we're finally going to get to see him live in concert."

"Oh, this is just magical", Jamie says. "The Math Club dies on their first adventure."

"Hey, you used the name!"

"Shut up."

I look at Kelly. She surprisingly seems calm and stoic as usual.

"What do we do?" I ask.

"We fight", Kelly says.

"What?" Jamie says.

I sigh. "I guess we'll never know how high the sycamore grows."

"What?"

"Never mind. Kelly, I don't like our odds in a fight."

I turn back towards the Zombsters. They're about twenty seconds away from us.

The evil, bloody version of Kenny laughs at us as we await our impending death.

I turn back to Kelly who is stretching out for some reason.

"You're serious about us fighting?"

She responds by pulling a sword out of her back pocket.

I stand in amazement. "Very resourceful, but what are you going to do with that?"

"Everybody get out of my way!" She says.

Jimmy and Kelly both jump to the ground

"Do you know how to use that thing?" I ask Kelly.

"Get out of the way Eric."

She pushes me to the ground. I land on a soft rock and feel a sharp pain on my elbow.

I look up in time to see Kelly attacked by two Zombsters. She doesn't show much hesitation in pushing the first one of them off. I than see her swing her sword with the same thrust and swing move I had seen Reece do at the warehouse. The zombster wails in pain and flies to the ground.

But the rest of them are closing in fast! She dodges one and slices another. The sword is moving at an uncanny speed as it catches another Zombster in a vital organ.

Reece must have taught her everything he knows.

One of them manages to run past her.

"Run!" She screams to Jimmy and Jamie who jump from the ground and begin running in the other direction.

As they run away, I see Kenny standing by a gravestone, laughing. I get up and run towards him.

"Kenny! I'm not going to let you get away with this!"

Kenny steps forward into the light and I see his face is still dripping blood.

I stop dead in my tracks and begin stepping back.

"Hey Kenny, can't we talk about this?"

"I'm going to disintegrate you!"

He walks towards me.

"Hey Kenny, you forgot the third rule in a crisis situation."

"What's that?"

"I don't know. I never saw the end of that movie either."

"I'm going to eat you alive!"

I keep stepping back. I'm going to have to make a b-line towards the parking lot.

I turn to run and stumble right into somebody.

"Reece!"

"It appears that I've come at just the right time."

"Man, am I'm glad to see you."

He takes his sword out.

"Kenny", he says. "You didn't use the word disintegrate properly in that last sentence you said. The English language should be respected, and not tainted by the likes of you."

"Shut your face!" Kenny yells.

"Why don't you come over here and make me."

Kenny charges towards us.

Reece stands with the sword in his hand as I jump out of the way.

Kenny at full speed lunges at Reece.

At that moment Reece drops the sword.

"What are you doing?

He winds his arm back and punches the incoming Kenny right in the face.

Kenny does a full summersault flip to the ground.

Reece shakes his hand.

"You got blood on my hand", he says calmly.

Kenny quickly jumps to his feet and charges at Reece again. This time, Reece lifts his leg and catches Kenny with a high kick to the face.

"Oooo wow", I say. "That's that Tony Jaa shit!"

Kenny stumbles backwards and falls to one knee. He looks angry as he gets to his feet and points a finger at us.

"This isn't over! We'll meet again you bastard!" Kenny runs away into the darkness.

Reece takes off running towards the darkness.

"What are you doing?" I call to him.

"He has the book! I'm going to follow him", I hear Reece yell back.

He disappears into the darkness.

I stumble over to where Kelly stands.

"What happened to Jimmy and Jamie?"

Kelly shakes her head.'

"They're gone. They ran."

"Did they get away?"

"I think so. I'm not sure to be honest."

"Oh man, this is bad. Reece went after Kenny. I'm glad you called him."

"I didn't"

"How did he know we were here?"

"He followed us from the party."

"He was there?"

"He was our backup plan."

My cell phone rings. I pick it up immediately.

"Jamie, where are you?"

"We're at IHOP."

"Did any zombsters follow you?"

She is breathing hard. "No I don't think so. We ran through the woods."

"Ok good. I'm glad you guys are safe."

"Are you guys alright"

"Yeah, luckily Reece showed up. He went after the book."

"So what do we do now?"

"You guys? Nothing. Listen, I shouldn't ever have involved you. You could have been hurt and it would have been my fault."

"So you want us to just go to Homecoming and act as if everything is normal?"

"There is nothing else you can do. We'll do everything we can to get the book back. I'll update you tomorrow, but just proceed if nothing is going on."

She doesn't answer for a moment. "Ok. Just be careful."

"I will, talk to you tomorrow."

I hang up the phone.

"Now what?" I look at Kelly.

"We wait to hear from Reece", she answers.

15

I walk with Kelly on a rocky sidewalk down her street. She is quiet, distant as usual. There has to be a way to get past this wall she has in front of her.

"Were you born detached?"

She stops walking.

"I'm sorry?"

"I didn't mean that. But you always seem to be off on another planet."

"You've only known me a few days."

"Sure. I mean I understand if you're always thinking about other stuff. I do that sometimes."

"Bad habits die hard."

"So I've known you for a few days, but every time see I you I feel like we've just met."

"What do you mean?"

"I mean that you're such a closed book that it doesn't feel like

I've gotten to know you."

"What do you want to know?"

"Well, so far I know that you're withdrawn, and that you have the sword skills of Zorro."

"Reece is a good teacher."

"I can see that. So what are you like when you're not saving the town?"

She starts walking again, as do I. She doesn't look at me though, electing instead to stare straight ahead.

"Like a caterpillar."

"Explain to me how you're like a caterpillar."

"You know how a caterpillar turns into a butterfly, and how extroverted people call themselves social butterflies?"

"Oh. So you haven't come out of your cocoon yet. But why would you want to be extroverted?"

"I don't want to simplify it to just being extroverted. But there is more to life than reading books."

"Hey, you think so, but who knows?"

"You can read about adventures over and over again, but if your life has no adventure, it's kind of empty."

"I'm just about adventured out after the last few days."

She walks quickly. I have to speed up my pace to keep up with her.

"What's so bad about a quiet life of reading books?" I ask.

"It's not bad, it's just tedious. I think it would be good to do that kind of thing when we're old and grey, but not when we're young."

"So then you do enjoy all this action adventure stuff."

"I don't enjoy it. But what would I be doing if I wasn't doing this?"

"Reading books I suppose. Hey, do you want to hear a joke?"

"Is it funny?"

"It's right off the top of my head, so I can't really judge the level of humor it contains."

"Let's hear it."

"Alright, so Vin Diesel has a twin brother. What is his name?"

"I don't know."

"Guess."

"I honestly have no idea."

"Twin Diesel."

"What?"

"Lame, I know. Ironically, however, it's true that he has a twin brother."

"You know, you remind me of a friend I used to have."

"Was he a sharp dresser with an amazing wit?"

"No, but he was on the chess team."

"Oh. Well, nothing wrong with that."

We come to what I'm guessing is her house a moment later. She stops on the front porch.

"This is my house."

"Will your parents care about you being out this late?"

"It's just me and mom that live here."

"Oh."

"She doesn't care about me being out late as long as I'm keeping my grades up."

"Do you?"

She nods.

"I don't know how. I don't go to class that often. I guess reading those books pays off."

"It can't hurt. I used to read a lot as a kid, but I guess somewhere along the way I got sucked into the internet world. But I have read every single RL Stine book possible."

"RL Stine?"

"Hey we can't all read Gone with the Wind. "

"Yes but RL Stine?"

"You have to start somewhere."

"I started with Ernest Hemmingway."

"I didn't know you were a braggart. So I remember you said I was a loner. What about you?"

She stares ahead blankly before responding.

"I don't trust people."

"That's fair. Did some guy break your heart?"

"You could say that."

"I think teenagers embody the word untrustworthy."

"What reason do you have to not be trusting?"

"Well I can't say any girl broke my heart, but the people at school can't be trusted."

"How do you know?"

"I just do."

"Do you really know, or are you just saying that."

"Maybe not through personal experience, but I've seen the rumors that have gone around about others."

"But personal experience is what counts. How do you know how things are unless you experience them for yourself?"

"That sounds like a good justification to take drugs."

"No I mean with people, you know, why judge them?"

It's an eye opening statement she has made.

"Perhaps. Hey are you going to college next year?"

"Community college, my mom can't afford anything else. What about you?"

"I don't know. I can barely bring myself to go to class these days."

"Everybody has their own path they have to take."

"You know, everybody I tell that too just gives me a generic lecture about how college is the only answer."

"Yeah but you have to live your own life."

"It's hard to do that when you live at home and are completely reliant on your parents."

"That's a benefit to going away for college."

"Wow, you're different than everybody."

She looks down. "No, I'm not."

"I think you are."

She looks up at her house.

"I better go."

She turns to leave.

"Wait", I say.

"Yes?"

"If Reece solves this thing, I mean if everything is good to go for Homecoming tomorrow."

"Yes?"

"Do you want to go?"

"You mean, together?"

"Well it doesn't have to be a date. I mean I want to experience a school dance for once. I guess I just don't want to do it alone."

"That's cute."

"I'm not sure if cute is what I'm going for."

She thinks for a moment although her facial expression doesn't change even slightly.

"I will go to the dance with you."

My face meanwhile naturally forms into a broad smile.

"Excellent. But one thing though, I can't really afford a tux, or a limo, or anything. I'll get flowers though."

"That stuff doesn't mean anything to me."

"I'm kind of like Leo on the Titanic, where he didn't have a dollar in his pocket and had nothing to offer Rose but he still won her over."

"But you don't look like Leo."

"Ouch."

"I'm joking. You're too easy."

"So as long as we stop a demon from destroying everybody, we should have a good time."

"Pick me up at seven."

"I'm looking forward to it."

16

I walk into my house about fifteen minutes later. I tip-toe up the stairs so as to not wake my parents and stagger into my room and collapse onto the bed. It's been a long day and I really just want to pass out. But my computer monitor screen is on. I hate having any type of light on when I'm sleeping. I maneuver myself off the bed and into the computer chair. I reach to turn off the monitor but I notice something troubling. Microsoft word is open and there is message on the screen.

"**Eric**?"

What the hell.

I lean back in my computer chair. I decide to humor my computer and type a response.

"This is him. Who are you?"

It takes only a moment for a response to appear.

"**Sandra**."

I remember Reece's story, and also that Sandra used to live in my house.

"Don't take this as anything sarcastic, but are you the Sandra from the eighties? The one who used to live here?"

"**Yes.**"

My hands freeze on the keyboard. I realize I'm messaging a dead person.

"So that you would make you dead. How are you communicating with me?"

"**I am in a world that sits between the living and the afterlife. The victims of Magra cannot rest until he is killed.**"

"Did you send the letters to Reece"?

"**Yes. I knew that he would be the one to help stop Magra. I've followed Reece from this side, ever since that night. I know he's tried hard to figure out what happened.**"

"So are you up to speed with what's going on?"

"**Yes. I am in your head.**"

"What do you mean?"

"**Since I knew that Reece would ask you for help, I thought I could slip into your head and see your thoughts. I believed that I could influence you to help out.**"

"How long have you been able to see all my thoughts?"

"**A few days.**"

"Are you the reason why I suddenly wanted to go to Homecoming?"

"**Yes. A little bit. The truth is that your thoughts were already welcome to the idea of helping out Reece before I influenced them.** "

"I guess I was waiting for something to happen in my life."

"**It didn't take much influence from me to set you on the path.**"

"Maybe you can help us. What do you know about Magra?"

"**He was once a student, someone who wasn't treated very well by the others.**"

"So killing people at the dance, it's some kind of revenge angle?"

"**Yes. Magra is trying to punish the popular students.**"

"And there are always popular kids at the dances."

"**Yes.**"

"Is the dance the only place he can appear?"

"Every demon has a portal way into our world. The gym at Dale Bridge High is Magra's. It's the only place he can enter into our world. And he has to have people he can possess."

"Anything else you can tell me about him?"

"He's big on art."

"Ok. But is he restricted in any way?"

"It takes a lot out of Magra to appear in front of humans or possess them. He can usually only possess the world of the living for a few minutes before his energy is depleted and he has to go away and recover."

"That's a relief. Is there a way to send him away for good?"

"The spell will send him away forever."

"And then your soul can rest?"

"Yes."

"Where did the spell come from?"

"We don't know. It's always been around, but Magra has made sure that it never got into the wrong persons hands. The type of person who could use it to end him."

"You mean Reece?"

"Yes."

"He was really taken with you."

"Yes, and I regret that I never got to tell Reece how I felt. But he's moved on, as the living must always do."

"How do you know he's moved on?"

"It's not my place to say, but maybe you'll find out someday."

"You were around the first time. If we can't stop Magra, how bad is it going to be?"

"If you can't get the spell, it will be devastating, and not just for the people at the dance."

"Wait, what do you mean by that?"

"Magra isn't just looking to kill people at the dance anymore. Recently he's found a way to sustain his energy level."

"For how long?"

"Long enough."

So what are you saying?"

"Once Magra is done with the students at the dance, he's going to move onto the rest of the town. And it won't stop there."

"Wait a minute, what are we talking about here?"

"If someone doesn't read that spell and send Magra away. It may be the end of the world."

17

CRACK!

I awake to the awkward sound of a rock hitting my window. I rub my eyes and stumble out of bed and make my way down the stairs. It's definitely morning.

"Who is there?" I say when I get to the front door.

"It's Reece."

I open it and see Reece standing there.

And he's not alone.

"Whoa", I say.

Reece pushes Kenny into my house. His hands are tied behind his back and he has a sock shoved in his mouth. He falls to the ground as Reece follows inside and shuts the door behind him.

"What time is it?" I ask.

"Dawn", Reece answers.

"So I guess you caught Kenny."

"Yes I followed him through the night. He mostly stayed in public places, but I caught him in the Waffles Galore parking lot about an hour ago."

"You haven't slept all night?"

"No", Reece says as I note the dark brown circles under his eyes.

Kenny tries to mumble something but nothing clear comes out.

"So what now?" I ask.

"We make him talk", Reece says.

I look down at Kenny and then back at Reece.

"Are we going to torture him?"

"Maybe, why do you ask?"

"My parents are upstairs sleeping. I think someone getting tortured in the living room may wake them up."

Reece looks around for a moment and then settles his stare on the back door.

"Would you prefer to do this in the backyard?"

"That would be better."

Reece picks Kenny up and carries him towards the back door. I open it half way and wait until they walk through before stepping through and closing the door. It is a bright, sunny day as we make our way to the middle of my backyard. Reece again pushes Kenny to the ground. This time he bends over and takes the sock out of Kenny's mouth.

"You bastards!" is the first thing that comes out of Kenny's mouth.

Reece slaps him.

"Did I give you permission to speak you schmuck?" Reece says.

I look around to make sure none of the neighbors are out on their deck enjoying morning coffee.

"Tell us where the book is", Reece says.

"Never!" Kenny answers.

I tap Reece on the shoulder and lean into his ear.

"He seems pretty stern on not giving us the book. Are we really going to torture him?"

Reece bats an eye. "It may be the only way."

"We can't kill him though right?"

Reece doesn't answer me. He instead turns back to Reece.

"You are forcing my hand here", he says quietly.

"Get away from me!"

"Are you going to cut off his legs with your sword?"

Reece shakes his head. "A cop was watching me earlier; I had to ditch the sword."

"What?"

"I have a backup, just not with me."

"So how are we going to torture him?"

Reece look around. "I have some ideas", he says.

He walks towards my deck and begins looking under it.

While he's doing that, I bend down over Kenny.

"This is going to be bad if you don't tell us where the book is."

Kenny grunts. "He won't hurt me."

"Trust me; he will do anything to stop Magra."

"I thought you assholes were supposed to be the good guys?"

"There are no good guys and bad guys. Just people in control and people who are getting tortured."

I hear the loud sound of an engine revving up. And I realize immediately what it is.

"What is that?" Kenny asks frantically.

"We're about to find out how strong your allegiance to Magra is."

Reece slowly walks towards us with the revved up lawnmower.

I'm just hoping my parents think it's the neighbor mowing their yard.

"What is he doing?" Kenny asks me.

Reece stops about three feet short of Kenny's face.

"Tell him to stop", Kenny pleads with me.

"Why should I? You never gave me back my Madden!"

Reece stands behind the lawnmower and shouts to me.

"Step out of the way Eric. I'm going to run over Kenny's face!"

I look down at Kenny and see his eyes just about bulge right out of their sockets in fear.

"Tell us where the book is or your face is going to look like a thin crust pizza."

"I can't! Magra will kill me!"

Reece takes a step forward with the lawnmower. The noise of the lawnmower makes me speak louder.

"Weight your options Kenny! I would say the lawnmower is the more immediate problem for you here."

Kenny shakes his head as Reece again moves forward towards his face.

"He's getting closer!" I shout.

Reece is now one step away from Kenny's face. He takes the step and lifts the front of the lawnmower and holds it directly over Kenny's face.

"Last chance!" I yell.

Reece begins to lower the front of the lawnmower towards his face.

I turn away, not wanting to see what's about to happen.

"Wait I'll tell you!!"

I hear Kenny scream that at just the right moment. Luckily for him Reece hears the scream over the revved up engine. The lawnmower shuts down.

"Saved by the confession", Reece says.

He picks Kenny up.

"Take me to where the book is immediately."

Kenny breathes hard as he manages to say "It's in my locker you psycho."

Reece looks at me.

"I'll notify you when I get the book."

"Ok, but instead of the walkie talkie why you don't you just call my cell phone."

"Right."

"Reece, are you sure we shouldn't just try to get the dance canceled?"

"No. Either way we're going to have to be there to say that spell. It will be easier for us to have access if the dance is going on. This is our only choice."

It's an hour before the homecoming dance and I'm standing outside of Kelly's house. Reece called me earlier in the day to tell me that he had the book in his possession. That takes some of the edge off our situation although there is still the matter of confronting Magra and vanquishing him with the spell.

For now, I'm doing my best to enjoy my very first Homecoming dance. I don't have a tux but I'm wearing a nice dress shirt and tie. My first ever non clip-on actually. I half expected Kelly's mother to invite me in for pictures but all I've gotten is a text from Kelly saying she'll be outside in a moment.

The door opens and she walks out onto the porch. I'm actually stunned to see her wearing a typical blue homecoming dress. I had some doubt in my mind that she would go all out in a traditional way.

"You look very elegant", I say.

She looks down at her dress and back at me with a serious expression.

"My mom bought it for me last year."

"Were you planning at some point to go to a dance?"

"I think my mom hoped that I would. So you're wearing a suit?"

"Yes, well, Burlington Coat Factory had a sale."

"Not bad", she says.

We step off the porch and walk down the driveway.

"Which car do you want to take?" I ask.

She shrugs her shoulder. "Does it matter?"

"I think its tradition to go in the guy's car."

"Is it?"

"I don't know but it sounds right."

"So let's take your car."

She starts to walk towards my car but I freeze.

"Wait", I say.

"What?"

"Tradition aside, I have a crappy Honda Civic and you have an Acura RSX. Maybe we should take your car."

"Ok."

We walk towards her car.

"Hey if you let me drive it will still let me save face and feel like a man."

She puts her keys in the lock and looks at me.

"Sure. Can you drive stick?"

"Damn."

I open the passenger door and get in.

The Homecoming Dance is held every year in the Dale Bridge High gymnasium. As we walk in past the big double door entrance I notice blue and red decorations have been planted all over the gym. Many of the students are already on the dance floor and I notice Mr. Edwards is standing over by the stage with a clipboard in his hands.

"Are you excited for your first dance?" Kelly asks.

I laugh.

"Just you saying that makes me feel like I'm eleven years old."

The gym is crowded with what I would guess is at least half the school. I spot Tracy standing over by the stage, but no sign of Kenny who was supposed to be her date.

I see Jamie and Jimmy standing off to the side. We approach and Jamie's eyes light up.

"Wow! You guys actually dressed up."

"I mean we are high school students", I say in response.

Jimmy gives a slight nod in acknowledgement.

"Kelly, can you come to the girl's room with me?"

"I guess", Kelly says as Jamie grabs her by the hand and drags her away.

I'm left standing next to Jimmy.

"Not a big dancer?" I ask.

"You could say that."

"Listen, I want to apologize to you about something."

He raises an eyebrow. "What are you talking about?"

"I've been kind of a hater, I mean in regards to you dating Jamie."

He doesn't react as he takes a sip of punch he has in his hands.

"I know you guys are best friends", he says.

"That's the thing; I think I was just looking out for her. I mean you have this reputation and I was just going by that instead of…"

"Instead of actually talking to me and seeing what I'm really about?"

"Yeah, I guess so."

"Sometimes when I'm around my boys I have to act a certain way. But, that doesn't mean I'm that way all the time."

"That makes sense. Listen if it means anything at all, which by all means it's ok if it doesn't, you and Jamie have my full support. I can see she really cares about you and I think the feelings are mutual."

He nods. "Yeah, they are."

I lean against the wall with him. He takes another sip of his punch.

"So this doesn't mean we have to hang out or anything right?" He says.

"No, I think this was fine."

I get up from the wall and walk away.

"Son! Guess whose DJ'ing this mothasucka!"

I see Dan Fundell standing behind the DJ table with a giant pair of headphones hanging from his neck.

"Wow, I like this setup you have here", I say.

"Yo its crazy son. I'm about to jump start this party!"

He reaches for his IPOD and then grabs the microphone.

"Yo party scrubs", he screams into the microphone. "Get ready to dance your Air Jordan's off!"

He presses a button and a song starts to play on the speakers throughout the gym.

Its N Sync's "Tearing Up My Heart"

"Yeah son!!" Dan screams. "How ya like them apples Dale bridge?"

A tomato hits him in the face from out of nowhere. It explodes and bits of it fly onto his IPOD.

He wipes the tomato sauce from his face and grabs the microphone.

"Yo whoever threw the tomato, I'm coming for you son!"

He jumps from behind the turntable and walks off furiously.

I walk by the entrance and am suddenly grabbed and pulled outside.

"Reece, you scared me."

He is wearing a dress shirt and pants. I suppose trying to pass as a chaperone.

"Have you seen anything suspicious in there?" He asks.

"You mean outside of the fact that they're letting Dan Fundell be the DJ?"

"Last time, Magra waited until after the homecoming king and queen ceremony before showing himself."

"You think history will repeat itself?"

"We have to assume so."

"So what's the plan?'

"Well Magra is going to try to possess somebody, but we don't know who. I'm going to slip in there and keep eye on everything."

"You have the spell right?"

"It's three words, and I have them memorized?"

"Why memorize it?"

"I'm going to destroy the page that holds the spell."

"What, why?"

"The spell can get rid of Magra, but that same spell if repeated a second time would bring him back."

"Damn. Ok we should absolutely destroy it then."

"As soon as he possesses somebody, I'll say the spell loud and clear."

"Ok, I'm going to go see if Kelly wants to dance."

He stops me and raises an eyebrow.

"You like Kelly?" He asks

"I think so."

He looks very serious as he nods his head.

"Do not hurt her."

"Well she would actually have to reciprocate my feelings before we get to that point."

He remains silent and so I turn around.

"I'll keep you updated if I see anything weird going on."

As I walk back in I see Kelly standing by the punch bowl looking bored. I walk over and pour myself a glass before standing next to her.

"I got an update from Reece. He wants us to continue to proceed as normal."

"And what is normal?" She asks.

I look out to the many students on the dance floor.

"I guess this is all normal."

She nods and looks ahead also.

"They all seem to be having a good time."

I see Jamie and Jimmy dancing, surprising since I didn't picture him to be the dancing type. To be fair he's more swaying from side to side and snapping his fingers than anything else.

"Well, we're dressed the part, what do you say we act it?"

She looks at me as if I'm crazy.

"Are you asking me to dance?"

"That was my intention, yes."

"Have you ever danced before?"

"I did a mean Macarena when I was a kid."

"I can sort of picture that."

"So you'll dance then?"

She looks onto the dance floor again and then all around the gym. She may be noticing what I'm noticing, that we are the only ones at the dance who aren't out on the floor busting a move.

"Yes, let's dance", she says finally.

We walk onto the floor awkwardly looking for an open spot.

"This seems fine", I say as we stop near the middle.

It's just as we hit the spot that 'Endless Love' by Luther Vandross and Mariah Carey starts playing. I put my hands on her waist although from the look on her face I don't think she was expecting a slow dance. My hands sit on her waist but her arms stay by her side.

"Have you slow danced before?" I ask.

"No, but I've seen it in just about every romance movie."

"You watch romance movies?"

"Is there something wrong with that?"

"No, not at all. I just didn't take you for the romantic type."

She sighs and finally puts her arms up on my shoulders.

We move from side to side. It takes me a moment to get over the fear of tripping and falling to the ground. Soon though I settle in and get comfortable. Kelly seems pretty loose also. Maybe I'm terrible at picking up on the signs, but I still haven't been able to detect how she feels about me.

"So this is what dancing at Homecoming feels like", I say.

"Do you feel like one of the popular kids?"

"Honestly, there are a lot more non popular kids here than I would have expected. I don't think Homecoming is about being popular, it's about just being a teenager and having fun."

"So maybe you were overthinking it?"

"I do that sometimes."

Over Kelly's shoulder, I see Jamie looking at us dancing with a surprised face. She gives me a thumbs up.

"So", I say. "There is something I wanted to ask you about."

"What is it?"

"The light jacket, you never told me what the deal with that is."

She nods.

"You know how I live with my mother?"

"Yeah."

"I never met my father."

"Really?"

"My mom got pregnant with me by accident. She never told my father about me until a few years ago."

"Wow, that's heavy."

"My mom said my father was someone who didn't want any attachments. She's never given much of an explanation beyond that."

"I'm sorry."

She takes a long sigh.

"On my birthday last year, I got this jacket in the mail. There was no return address, but I had this feeling my father sent it."

"I understand why it's so important to you than."

'Endless Love' ends just then. Everybody on the floor separates as the music stops.

"That wasn't so bad", I say.

The song 'All for You' by Sister Hazel begins to play.

I wonder if we should leave the dance floor but Kelly starts moving with the music along with everyone else. I start moving also although without any sense of rhythm.

"I wish I could dance better", I try to say over the music.

"Why are you snapping your fingers?" She says back.

"I have no idea", I say as I stop snapping.

"I like this song", she says.

"Yeah, this is like the happiest song of all time."

"What do you mean?"

"I swear I've seen this song play over the trailer of like every other romantic comedy in the last ten years."

She smiles.

"Now that has to be the first time I've seen you smile."

'All for You' suddenly cuts off.

Kelly looks around. "Why didn't the song finish?"

"I'm not sure."

I look towards the DJ table and notice that nobody is there.

"I don't see anyone controlling the music", I say.

Suddenly, the song 'Vincent' by Don Mclean starts to play throughout the gym.

We look around and see the other students standing around dumbfounded. 'Vincent' is neither a slow song or fast paced. I'm actually pretty certain that most of the students here haven't heard it.

"Something's not right here", Kelly says.

"I have something on the tip of my mind", I reply and I think long and hard about what it is.   The song continues to blast through the gym speakers.

"Now I understand what you tried to say to me, and how you suffered for your sanity. And how you tried to set them free. They did not listen they did not know how. Perhaps they'll listen now.."

And it hits me, suddenly and fierce.

"It's happening", I say.

Kelly shakes her head. "How do you know?"

"Sandra told me that Magra is a fan of art. This song is about Vincent Van Gough!"

The Double doors fly open. And Kenny walks in with three zombsters right behind him.

19

A few of the students scream loud at the sight of the zombsters. Mostly, they all gather together and back up towards the stage area. Mr. Edwards is standing along with the students and he looks just as shocked and scared as them.

Kenny stands in front of them and puts his hands in the air.

"Everybody, welcome to the end of the world!" He yells.

"Can you keep him talking?" Kelly asks.

"I can try, but where are you going? And where is Reece?"

"I don't know, but I have to get my sword from my locker before he locks us all in."

"Well what if those things attack us while you're away?"

"If they wanted to attack they would have already done it. I think he's just trying to keep everyone here until Magra takes over."

Kenny begins to lock the double doors behind him. It seems Kelly is right in that he just wants to keep us here for the slaughter.

She takes off towards the side exit.

Kenny is still chain locking the double doors so I run over to Dan Fundell.

"Dan, I need a favor. I need you to get on the microphone and calm everyone down."

"Son this is mind blowing! What do you want me to say?"

"I don't know, just try to keep them calm."

"I got you son!"

He runs back to his DJ booth and grabs the microphone.

"Umm yo, like, attention ladies and students. Give me your attention bitches!"

The screaming stops and the students get quiet for a second.

Dan hesitates for a moment before speaking.

"Yo, we're all going to die he's going to kill us one by one!"

The students scream in terror.

"Stupid", I say to myself as I make my way towards Kenny. He laughs at the site of me.

"Poor Eric", he says. "Are you still trying to play yourself off as some type of hero?"

"You mean like how you're still trying to play yourself off as some type of villain?"

"Eric, you don't have a hamster in this fight."

"You mean dog?"

"No I mean a hamster you moron. Forget dogs!"

"You're making a mistake Kenny. You think once Magra is done with all of us he's just going to let you go free? He wants to take over the world you know."

"And I would rather be on his side than against him."

"So where is your great master huh? What, did he stop at a Dunkin Doughnuts drive through? What is he waiting for?"

"Oh he'll be here shortly."

A hand grabs my shoulder. "We better work fast than", someone says.

I turn and see Reece standing next to me with a sword. Kelly is with him also.

"You", Kenny says pointing at Reece.

"You didn't learn your lesson from this morning?" Reece says.

"This time it's going to be an even fight", Kenny answers.

He pulls out a sword.

"That's right. I have a sword too."

Reece smirks and then turns to Kelly. "Go over with the other students. If these zombsters get past me, you're the last line of defense."

Kelly nods and then looks at me. "Be careful", she says.

"You know, in hindsight, you guys probably should have taken a few minutes out to show me how to use a sword. I'm just saying."

She jogs away.

"I'll make quick work of Kenny", Reece says. "I need you to get to that door and try to unlock it. We need to try to get the students out of here before Magra arrives."

"What about the zombsters?" I ask.

Reece shakes his head. "I didn't expect them", he says.

"We got em", I hear a voice say.

I turn and see Jimmy and the J-Gang standing next to us. Jimmy has a baseball bat in his hand and the other two members have hockey sticks.

"I'm impressed", I say. "But I have to warn you guys, this isn't going to be the same thing as taking lunch money from freshman."

"I brought the J-Gang up to speed", Jimmy says. "They know what's at stake."

"No more talk", Kenny yells. "It's time to die!"

The three Zombsters run at us and Jimmy immediately swings and catches one of them in the face with a swing that would make Sammy Sosa proud.

Kenny charges at Reece with the sword. Reece ducks Kenny's swing with his sword and fires back but Kenny surprisingly is able to counter with a few moves of his own.

The J-Gang are doing a good job of holding off the zombsters as I duck down and try to move around all the fighting. I make my way to the door and find that it's locked with a steel chain. Great, how am I supposed to open this?

I look back at the fighting just in time to see Reece hit Kenny in the chin with the handle part of the sword. Kenny flies to the ground and immediately begs for mercy. Reece kicks his sword away from him and then turns his attention to the zombsters. The J-gang has been holding them off but I can see they are starting to get tired.

With a swift and quick swing, Reece slices one of the zombsters in half. He then puts his sword right through the throat of a second one. There is only one remaining and he's very aware that Reece has killed his buddies. Jimmy and the J-Gang head back towards the crowd of other students as Reece squares up the final zombster.

The zombster yells something in a different language and lunges at Reece. The Zombster's head is separated from his body a quick instant later.

Reece starts to slip his sword into his pocket and that's when I see it.

Kenny behind Reece, holding a knife that he must have had hidden.

"Reece, behind you", I yell. I run as fast as I can.

But it's too late. Kenny slips the knife into Reece's side.

I tackle Kenny just then. Since I don't have a weapon I begin choking him.

My goal is to choke him out but he manages to slap me on the side of head and knock me off of him.

He stands up and inches towards me with the knife.

"Say goodbye Mckay", he says.

He raises the knife high ahead of his head and prepares to bring it down on me.

But the bottom of Reece's sword catches him hard right on the back of his head.

He falls down, unconscious. Reece drops the sword and

crumbles to the ground.

"Reece", I say as I crawl over near him. "Are you alright?"

"No", he answers. "I'm losing too much blood."

"We just have to put pressure on it", I say as I take off my coat.

"No", he answers. "It's not important. We don't have much time."

"What do you mean?"

"The spell, I destroyed it. But I'm going to tell it to you. You have to recite it when Magra comes."

"C'mon man you're going to be fine. You can recite it yourself."

"Stop, you're wasting time. The spell is three words."

"Three words, ok."

"Memorize these words. Valenkna, Vamania, Vatricinia."

"Ok got it."

"Repeat them."

"Valenka, Vamania, Vatrincia. But you'll be able to say them yourself."

"Listen to me", he says and I hear his breathing become heavier.

"You have to lookout for Kelly."

"What do you mean?"

"There is something you don't know."

"What is it?"

His breathing is becoming heavier with every word.

"She is my daughter."

I look up from Reece and see Kelly coming over towards us.

"You mean you sent her the jacket?" I ask.

He nods. "Yes, the jacket belonged to Sandra."

"Listen, I'm going to get you to a hospital and you're going to be fine.'

"No!" he cries. "You have to stay and wait for Magra."

He turns his head and sees Kelly coming over. He looks back at me.

"Eric", he says almost in a whisper. "Don't tell her."

"I won't", I try to answer but I feel his body stop moving just as Kelly reaches us.

"Reece!" she cries and she comes to the ground and looks at him.

"He's gone", I say quietly.

"No, he can't be", she says. She shakes him and then puts her hand to her face.

I stand up and look back towards the students.

"He told me the spell", I say. "We have to wait for Magra to possess somebody and then I can say it and end this whole thing."

I start to walk towards the students when I hear Kelly behind me.

"You know the spell?"

"Yeah."

"Then I'll have to make sure I destroy your vocal cords."

"What?"

I turn back around and Kelly punches me right in the face.

20

She stands above me with an evil grin. Her green eyes have now turned bright red.

"Kelly what are you doing?"

"Who is Kelly", she replies.

She picks me up and throws me against the wall.

The rest of the kids scream and Magra looks at them with an annoyed expression.

"Stupid sheep", she says. She points a finger towards them.

"Sleep", she whispers.

I see all of the students suddenly fall to the ground. Magra must have put them under a spell.

Everyone except Mr. Ryan. He comes running over.

"Kelly, what are you doing? And what is wrong with your eyes?"

Magra turns towards Mr. Ryan.

"I have to warn you, I don't take well to authorities", she says.

"You're in big trouble missy", Mr. Ryan screams.

Magra lifts her hand and suddenly Mr. Ryan is up in the air.

"Go away", she whispers.

Mr. Ryan suddenly and violently flies across the room into the

DJ table. He doesn't get back up.

I feel a strong burning pain through my shoulders and back as I try to get back to my feet.

Magra turns her attention back to me.

"So Reece told you the spell. That makes you the only person who can stop me."

I stumble to my feet, breathing hard as she approaches me.

"That's right", I say. "I can stop you with three words."

"But will you?" She says with a cocky grin on her face.

"Why wouldn't I?"

"I've possessed your girlfriend's body. What do you think happens to her if you say that spell?"

"What are you saying?"

"It's not Algebra Eric; it's in fact very easy to figure out. You say those words, and Kelly dies."

"You're lying", I say.

"Then go ahead and say the words."

She stands in front of me.

Damnit! What do I do?

Magra's plan must have been to possess Kelly the whole time. Reece would have been the person to say the spell, but he wouldn't have done that if he knew it would kill Kelly. It was a great backup plan for Magra.

But Reece dying and passing the responsibility to me should be a big a dagger in Magra's plan.

The problem is I care about Kelly too.

Too much to say the words and kill her.

I hear laughing and see Kenny suddenly standing next to Magra.

"I told you Eric, you picked the wrong side."

He looks at Magra and smiles.

"Hey, maybe I can take you to the prom?"

Magra smiles.

She than grabs him by the head and cracks his neck.

He falls to the ground, lifeless.

"Hey, you killed Kenny!" I try to yell although it comes out more as a gasp than sentence.

She appears in front of me, grabbing me by the throat and pushing me against the wall.

"Poor Eric", she says. "You fall in love and find a purpose in your life, only to have to die. Talk about wrong place and wrong time!"

She lifts me up against the wall, her hands tightening around my throat.

"Sorry it has to end this way Eric", she says.

I feel the oxygen slipping away from my body and I begin to regret that I haven't lived a purposeful life until now.

Her hand tightens again, and only as I feel myself getting light headed do I realize what I have to do. I don't know if I have enough breath left to do it.

But I have to try.

I concentrate like I never have before.

And I think to myself, I'm sorry Kelly.

But Magra tightens her grip.

I mouth the words.

"Valenkna, Vamania, Vatrimia."

She doesn't react, infact she tightens her grip.

If the spell isn't working, I'm a goner.

But then I see it.

The confident look on her face begins to wither away, slowly but surely.

She lets go of me and begins to hold her throat.

I drop to the ground and struggle to catch my breath.

As I look up, I see the dark red in Kelly's eyes begin to fade out very slowly.

She looks at me, angry and in disbelief.

She is probably wondering how this slacker on academic probation has foiled her plans to rule the world.

She stumbles a few steps backwards and opens her mouth and a bright shining light suddenly shoots out of it and goes all the way through the ceiling.

I hear cries and gasps from the other students.

The light lasts for about twelve seconds before it disappears completely.

And Kelly falls to the ground.

I start to catch my breath and I move toward her.

"Kelly", I say slowly as I put my hand on her arm.

She isn't moving.

Jamie comes running over.

I look up at her.

"I don't know if she's alive", I say.

Jamie comes to the ground and puts her head to Kelly's heart.

I wait anxiously.

Jamie looks at me.

"She's alive."

I sigh in relief and fall onto my back next to Kelly.

I lay there and look up at the ceiling until Kelly gains consciousness.

She turns and looks at me.

"Is it over?"

"I think so."

I look around and see all of the students begin to wake up.

A few minutes later we are standing by the punch table as police walk all around the gym asking people questions. As it turns out, the police got a tip earlier in the night about that warehouse where the Zombsters were. It was there they found Samanta, alive and well, tied up. I have a feeling it was Reece who tipped them off. Tracy won Homecoming queen although the ceremony seemed a bit meaningless after everything else that had happened.

I see Mr. Ryan being wheeled away on a stretcher.

"You better be in class on Monday!" He yells at me before he exits.

"So everybody was basically asleep", I say to Kelly who is sipping punch.

"We can just say we didn't know what was going on."

"And the swords?"

"I found it in the hallway. Everything else was self-defense."

"What about Kenny?"

"Did I kill him?"

"Magra did, not you. But we can blame the zombsters."

She sighs. I can see her eyes fixed on where they are putting Reece in a body bag.

"I can't believe he's gone."

"He would at least be happy to know that we finished his mission."

"I'm going to miss him. He was more than a friend, he was almost like, like...."

"Like a father?"

21

After the police are done questioning us, Kelly and I head back to my house.

"I think this is the beginning of a beautiful friendship", I say as I open my front door and we walk into my house.

We stroll into the kitchen and I brew us a cup of coffee.

"So I'm thinking on Monday you can start tutoring me in Algebra?"

She laughs.

"Hey", I say, "I can't graduate if I don't pass."

"You bring the coffee, I'll bring the books."

"So you do like me."

"Maybe a little."

"That's a good start. So what do you want to do tonight?"

"Go home and sleep."

"Ok but I have an enticing offer that you may not be able to refuse."

"What do you have in mind?"

"I'm thinking you can watch the rest of Pocahontas with me."

"I've seen it."

"I just have to watch the ending."

"You shouldn't."

"Why? Disney movies always put me in a feel-good mood"

"Pocahontas is a downer."

"What do you mean?"

"I don't want to spoil it for you."

We get the coffee and begin walking up the stairs.

"So you're saying it's not a happy ending?"

"Would that surprise you?"

"I mean it's just not typical for a Disney movie. Usually our main characters fall in love and live happily after."

"Usually."

We walk into my room. She takes a seat on my bed and I turn the TV on. I take a seat on the bed next to her. I push play on the remote and Pocahontas comes on.

"A disney movie without a happy ending. Maybe the world is ending afterall."

"Hey, can you turn off the computer monitor", she asks.

"Sure", I say.

I get off the bed and walk over to the computer.

I reach for the power button on the monitor but freeze when I see what's on the computer.

"Eric, it's me Sandra. Are you there?"

I sit down in the chair.

"Yeah, thanks for the help. It's all over."

"No, it isn't!"

"What do you mean?"

"You must have said the spell incorrectly! Magra is still alive!"

Could I have said the words wrong? If I did I would just have to find the spell and say it correctly when Magra comes back.

Kelly appears next to me.

Wait, did Reece say he destroyed the spell?

"What's wrong?" She asks.

I turn off the monitor and look at her.

"I think we better skip the prom this year."